PRAISE FOR
SEPARATE

"When a tragic industrial 'accident' is allegedly caused by menacing specters, Dr. Elmir, professor of paranormal studies, and Rojana Bensen, his feisty, free-wheeling research assistant, set out to document what really occurred. From the start, their efforts and inquiries are diverted by puzzling occurrences—and in Rojana's case, otherworldly encounters. This engaging, cleverly written ghost story will have special appeal for those who like quirky humor with their horror."

—Ellen Sherman, Author of *Into the Attic*

"Alan and Sairung Wright create a compelling, eerie, and unsettling world in *Separate*, with dangerous implications for the living. After the lines between here and the hereafter get blurred, the reader must hang on with both hands to make it to the end."

—Travis Klempan, Author of *Have Snakes, Need Birds* and *Hills Hide Mountains*

Separate

by Alan and Sairung Wright

© Copyright 2023 Alan and Sairung Wright

ISBN 979-8-88824-081-6

Published by

köehlerbooks™

3705 Shore Drive
Virginia Beach, VA 23455
800–435–4811
www.koehlerbooks.com

SEPARATE

A NOVEL

ALAN AND SAIRUNG WRIGHT

VIRGINIA BEACH
CAPE CHARLES

PART 1

Presences and Presentations

1

"MAE NAK?" SOMPOB whispered hesitantly. The wraith at the far end of his hallway did not react to Sompob's stutter step or question but instead stared soundlessly into the wall, motionless. Sompob dared to look carefully at the phosphorescent form. It was a man. Whoever it was or had been, it was not the homicidal Mae Nak of legend. He felt immense relief.

Two hundred years ago, Mae Nak had died during childbirth while her husband was away at war, fighting for his king. But she refused to leave this world. She greeted her husband when he returned from Bangkok as if nothing had happened. They lived together as a family for a time, the husband unaware that his wife and baby were no longer alive. When he finally discovered the truth, he fled. Infuriated, Mae Nak pursued her husband, tormenting and killing anyone who interfered with her search. It was said that a monk eventually trapped her spirit or shepherded her to the next plane, but people still saw her, and some Thais still feared her.

The profile of the figure before Sompob was definitely not that of Mae Nak. It was pointed, with unnaturally jutting features. The brow, nose, and chin protruded as if they had been torn by a fishing hook. Other details were difficult to see in the shadows and half-light of the hallway. A breeze shifted the trees outside the nearby window, and the sunset's rays flickered through the leaves. In that speckled light, the ghost's face momentarily appeared full and clear. The next instant, it was a cracked, incomplete mosaic with pieces missing from the temple, earlobe, and jowl.

Sompob slowed his breathing and forced his eyes to sweep

downward, to check the figure's clothing for identifying features. The various spirits of Thailand's many ghost tales reacted differently to people. Some peacefully disappeared when approached. Others, like Mae Nak, were murderous. He needed to know what sort this one was.

From its wispy, neck-length hair to its tattered sandals, the entire spirit shimmered with the same colorless light. The clothes were obviously foreign and old. A drape covered its chest, and Sompob could not help speculating. Perhaps the drape concealed cracked bones, flesh stretched paper thin, or globs of organs writhing with hungry, corpse-nibbling insects. The simple drape bore a cross with three dots around each end. It wasn't Buddhist and it wasn't Thai. *It might be Christian*, Sompob thought. Nothing about this spirit felt familiar, though. Thankfully, while it stood facing the wall, it was not threatening.

But then its head turned. Its eyes—or rather, its blackened sockets—landed on Sompob. Its face bore no sign of curiosity or confusion. This was not a lost soul seeking assistance. It was not the shadow of a man who had bound himself to the house through years of hard work, longing, or tragic victimization. The expression it wore was stern. When its lips parted as if to inhale, they stretched unnaturally into a toothless grimace. This ghost, Sompob realized, meant to condemn.

Sompob took a step back in horror. *Did I offend it?* The question was almost a prayer. *Did I fail?* He tried to lead a clean life and follow the Five Precepts. He felt no temptation to kill, steal, or sleep with other men's wives. Abstaining from drinking and swearing, on the other hand, were tougher to obey. Once or twice a week, after leaving work to struggle through hordes of fury-inducing Bangkok drivers, Sompob needed whiskey to soothe his post-commute tension. That was the worst vice he had committed. He couldn't remember doing anything truly improper, much less worthy of a curse, but his innocence did not prevent the sticky chill of fear from climbing out of his stomach and up the back of his throat. He tried to think. *What is the right chant, the right posture, the right thing to do?*

The fear in Sompob's gullet bubbled up and seized his brain, swapping rationality with frenzied panic. *Nothing is right. I have to get away. I have to get away.* He twisted his body and ran for the front door. He didn't get far. After two full strides, his joints jammed like a bike with a crowbar shoved between its spokes, slamming him onto the floor. He stayed conscious and soon wished he hadn't.

Pain pierced every corner of his body, invoking images of jagged ice encasing his tendons and bones. Paralyzed, he lay on his side with his head partially turned up toward the ceiling. He rolled his eyes wildly and found the shade was close, too close, and drifting even closer. It stopped right over his frozen body and stooped like a crime scene coroner. Overwhelmed with dread, Sompob knew he was being examined but couldn't process it. The ghost's history and origin no longer intrigued him. It had surrounded him. He was inside it, and it was inside him.

The door stood just two meters ahead. Knowing it was futile, Sompob tried reaching for the knob anyway. The expressionless wraith watched him desperately accomplish nothing.

Sompob was breathless in the agony of his discomfort; his lungs felt engorged with stinging, dry sand. He attempted to heave the grittiness out, to vomit his guts onto the floor. He couldn't. There was no relief. Every muscle in Sompob's body ached to move, but he was restrained by ice, sand, the veil of the wraith, and then darkness.

2

SCANNING THE GRAY lecture hall to assess his audience as the syllabus was being handed out, Zeb hoped that this first discussion would get a response from his students. If students showed an iota of willingness to explore and an inclination to believe, most likely the rest of the term would be lively and engaging. By the end of it, they might seriously reconsider their notions of the world around them. But if the students didn't play along and his prompts were met with silence, the whole quarter would likely be frustrating, with only a few seriously contemplating the course's main ideas.

Zeb always began the term with a few introductory questions before reviewing the inherently tedious course policies and expectations. "Why are zombies scary?"

"Zombies aren't scary," said one student.

"One isn't scary; it's a whole lot of zombies that's scary," replied another.

"Because they're dead. They're gross," a third suggested.

"Because they just keep comin'. They can't be stopped," added a fourth. A few heads around the room nodded in agreement.

"Because they'll eat you and turn you into a zombie," called out someone in the back. The hall went quiet.

"Okay," said Zeb. "They're scary because they're dead people that want to eat you, to turn you into a zombie, and there's a lot of them. Has anyone seen a zombie, or known anyone who has seen a zombie?" No one raised their hand. "Does anyone think zombies could be real? That is, if there aren't zombies walking around today, do you think there could be zombies in the future, if a virus mutated or an experiment went wrong?" A couple hands went into the air, hesitantly. That was a good sign; some students weren't too embarrassed to voice what they really thought. Zeb's hope for this term grew.

"And what about ghosts?" he asked. "Why are ghosts scary?"

"They're dead and gross too."

"They're really old, like hundreds of years."

"They can hurt you, but you can't hurt them," said one of the same students who had voiced an opinion on zombies. Expressions of general agreement spread throughout the room.

"So, what would be scarier to you: coming face-to-face with a zombie or a ghost?"

Zeb heard many overlapping claims of "A zombie!" and "A ghost!" He couldn't tell which was more popular.

"Let me ask the ghost voters first. Why do you think they're scarier?"

"They have powers. Ghosts can move things around and float through walls. Zombies can't. You can hide from zombies, you can kill zombies, but you can't hide from ghosts, and you can't kill them."

"Exactly," said someone from earlier.

Zeb asked, "Do ghosts really attack the living? Has anyone here seen a ghost, or known anyone who did?" Quite a few hands shot into the air, which Zeb expected. Most students who registered for Culture 209: Specters of the World were motivated by stronger influences than the university's multiculturalism requirement. Personal motivation was good. The students had to be motivated to endure Zeb's infamous reading schedule.

"Would anyone like to share their story? How about you?" Zeb nodded toward a woman in the front row.

"My great-great-grandmother," she said. "We see her in my grandparents' farmhouse, early in the morning. She just kind of walks around, but she disappears when anyone gets near."

"'When anyone gets near,' you said. So your family isn't scared of your great-great-grandmother's ghost? She's never attacked anyone?"

"No, I don't think so."

"When was the last time you saw her?"

"I've only seen her once, when I was a kid. My parents and I were staying there for the Fourth of July. It was dark, though, so I'm not sure. But my sister's seen her a few times."

"It's often dark when people see ghosts. Is that just coincidence, or is it because when people are tired and their vision is blurry from sleep, their eyes play tricks on them? Or are ghosts always around us, but, like stars in the sky, we can't see them unless it's dark?" Zeb paused to give the students a moment to think, then proceeded. "Are ghosts real?" Gesturing to the woman who had just shared, Zeb asked, "Who here believes her story?"

There were far more hands in the air this time; clearly more students thought ghosts were real than zombies. "So, what we know so far is that if ghosts are real, they don't always attack. And they can be scarier than zombies because if they did attack, we wouldn't be able to escape. What we'll talk—"

"I know one that attacked," a determined student cut in.

"That's what we'll talk about in the coming weeks," said Zeb, pressing on. "We'll compare cultural perceptions of specters and spirits, including what they are, how they behave, and how to get rid of them, as well as important ghost stories from around the world. Most of you here probably already know from the campus grapevine that I'm a true believer, and perhaps if you're not a believer now, you will be at the end of this term."

The classroom rustled from the shifting of several students.

"One reassurance I'd like to give you today is that ghosts cannot interact with us, and therefore, they cannot attack. Most ghost stories do not include attacks, and the stories of attacks that have been investigated have been proven false. Injuries from supposed attacks are self-inflicted, most often from the witnesses themselves running into furniture, not spirits hurling dinnerware. Don't lose sleep over the deceased wandering the halls of your dorms. You will not get attacked by departed alumni tonight or any other night."

"One attacked in Bangkok," the same determined student proclaimed, rising to her feet as she spoke.

"Nang Nak? Nang Nak has been—"

"It wasn't Mae Nak, and it wasn't self-inflicted. My cousin was nearly killed!"

The room fell silent. Aware of the importance of demonstrating that students could approach him with questions, Zeb attempted to cool the fire under the student's seat. "Maybe your cousin saw something brand new. Would you mind meeting me in my office after class, to tell me more?" He knew better than to debate an impassioned student without knowing a sighting's specifics.

"Yeah, okay." She slowly sat back down.

"Now, let's talk about what you all need to do to pass." Having postponed the argument, Zeb led the hushed class through his policies and expectations.

3

THE ANTICIPATED KNOCK on Zeb's office door came two hours after class had ended. Naturally, Zeb wasn't surprised by the student's claim. The Mae Nak shrine in Bangkok was a hub for believers as well as misinformation. But it was always best to approach new tales of encounters calmly. If witnesses felt comfortable enough to share their beliefs freely, Zeb could then educate them about which details were probable and which were impossible. Mentally prepared for confrontation, Zeb answered the knock, hoping to meet a student relaxed by two hours of reflection.

"Dr. Elmir, I'm Rojana Bensen. I go by Na. I—"

"Yes, your cousin. You said he was almost killed, right?" Zeb saw Na's expression change from anticipation to guarded disapproval. He chided himself for his eager greeting. "I'm sorry, I'm getting ahead of myself. Hello, Na, I'm glad you came. Let's start with what you know and what you think happened. Please sit down."

Zeb waited quietly for Na to take in the surroundings. His office fit the stereotypical definition of a college professor's office. It was just large enough for a computer desk with a wall-sized bookcase behind it. There were two mismatched, oddly shaped wooden chairs. One was for himself. Behind the visitor's chair stood a metal filing cabinet. The office did not have windows, but a movie poster for *The Smiling Ghost* hung where a window might have been. The tension in Na's face disappeared when she saw the grinning cartoon. She slid all the way back in her seat before speaking.

"A ghost attacked my cousin, Sompob Suetrong, two months ago. He saw it in his hallway, just after dinner. At first it didn't move, but then it stared right at him and chased him. He tried to run, but it caught him, and all he remembers before passing out is feeling pain all over. Some neighbors who were walking home heard a noise and went to check on him. When they opened his door, they found him lying on the floor. They called for an ambulance. When Sompob woke up at the hospital, he was stiff and had some strained muscles, but the doctors didn't find any injuries, and the tests all came back normal. It's not normal to be unconscious for that long, but they can't explain it.

"Now he's living with his parents. He doesn't want to go back home. He'd try to sell it, but no one in Bangkok will buy a haunted house. Everyone knows about his story now, so he's trying to decide what to do. That house is his investment. It's his savings . . ." She paused and looked down at her hands, her dark, shoulder-length hair hanging around her face like a curtain.

"Do you believe it? Without qualification?" Zeb asked gently.

Na glanced at the ancient movie poster. "I first heard about it from my parents, who had talked to his parents. But then I talked to him, and he's sure. He doesn't remember much, but he remembers its glow, and the fear and the pain. Sompob's smart, and he works hard. I believe him."

"Well, let me explain something quickly. This is simplifying things a bit, so take it with a grain of salt. When we see ghosts and they see us, it's like a video conference. Have you been at a video conference, or used a messenger program that lets you talk to someone using video? It's like that—a video conference without sound. Sometimes we can see them, and sometimes they can see us, but we're not actually in the same place. We can't reach out and touch their world. We can't grab them, and they can't grab us. The ghost may have come toward Sompob, it may have even passed through him, but nothing could have happened because they weren't in the same place. They weren't in the same world. Does that make sense?"

"Mmm, not really. If the ghost wasn't there with him, how did it hurt him?"

Zeb replied carefully, watching for changes in Na's expression. "That's the thing. I'm not convinced it did hurt him, at least physically. Okay, Sompob is trustworthy, you spoke to him and feel his story is genuine. It's absolutely possible that a ghost was in his house and the sight of it terrified him. It may have even moved in his direction. However, interaction is necessary for one being to hurt another—direct, physical interaction, which is either impossible or so rare that it's undocumented.

"It's far more likely that the pain Sompob felt was from fear and stress, which can cause cramping. Then, he panicked and passed out. That would explain his symptoms and loss of consciousness without an actual physical assault. Physical assaults, like I said in class, are unsupported. As far as we know, they've never happened before, so why would they start happening now?"

Na squared her shoulders and leaned forward. "But, Dr. Elmir, unsupported by who? Sompob supports them, others have supported them, like all the stories about Mae Nak. Just because *you* don't believe in ghost attacks doesn't mean they don't happen."

"From what you said, there were no witnesses, correct? How did the rest of your family react? Does everyone believe him with the same vigor you do?"

"His parents trust him, and my parents trust him, but no, not everyone does. Our uncle figures Sompob was punished for not repaying a loan. And one of the neighbors who found him said the house's previous owners had seen ghosts too, but they were never attacked. He thinks Sompob did something to upset the ghosts, like trying to chase them out, but now Sompob's embarrassed and won't say what really happened.

"Both of them are being stupid. My uncle thinks everything is about money, literally everything, so he's stupid about everything unless it really is about money. I don't understand what the neighbor is thinking. My relatives know him; they met before Sompob bought the house, and he didn't say anything then. They've eaten together on New Year's, had Songkran parties, and on and on. But all of a sudden, after this, he says the house has always been haunted? I don't know. Everyone who knows Sompob well trusts him. You should too." Her eyes pleaded with Zeb.

"It's not a matter of trust. It's a matter of probability. In all probability, things did not happen the way Sompob and you describe them. That's just a statement, not an affront. The pain, the loss of consciousness—that's just not how these things work.

"I'll tell you what. You'll all be doing a research project that counts for forty percent of your grade, remember? Physical contact between ghosts and people would make a great topic. Why don't you focus on that? You could get started right now. Search for information and examples. With a better understanding of these things, I think you'll find the solace you're after. And if you find something interesting, something that supports Sompob's version of what happened, you can show it to me. How does that sound?"

"Okay. Thanks for your *time*, Dr. Elmir," she said coldly. Na quickly rose and swept out of the office, rustling the papers on Zeb's desk and eliciting a crinkle from the poster hanging loosely on the wall. Zeb sighed at his indelicacy, attributing the amount of turbulence created by such a small person to his recent lack of rest.

WADE HAD ONLY taken a few steps onto the plant's manufacturing floor before he noticed something wrong. His coveralls flapped between his legs, and excess fabric around his waist kept his arms from swinging freely. "Hey, Jeff," he called to the plant manager on the other side of the conveyor, "give me a few minutes here." Spreading his legs and holding his arms up, he added, "Look how baggy this thing is. I'm a duck's foot!"

Jeff glanced up, smiled, and yelled back, "Yeah, alright. We're not ready yet anyway." Jeff returned his attention to the three workers next to him.

This was Wade's first day back at work in months. Pneumonia had almost taken his life. For a few weeks after calling the doctor but before his meds kicked in, he had wondered if he would live to retire. During those torturous days and nights, the sludge in his chest gurgled and bubbled with each breath, producing fizzing pain somewhere between muscle cramps and deep itches. The effort of breathing left him too weak to cook or go shopping. A bachelor from trial and error, he lived alone and had been forced to survive on the canned food he'd stored for emergencies and natural disasters. He had only recently regained enough health to prepare what he considered a nourishing meal. Consequently, he had lost so much weight that his coveralls were now unsafe to wear on the factory floor.

In terms of scheduling, it had been a good time to get seriously sick. The pneumonia hit just as the plant was shutting down for upgrades and heavy maintenance. Jeff and a few others saw the maintenance as an engaging change of pace. They enjoyed getting their hands on the bits of machinery they watched every day but couldn't touch. Wade, on the other hand, dreaded maintenance. To him, it meant lifting, pulling, crawling, and reaching into tight spaces. Worst of all, it meant getting grease all over his hands, in his hair, and on his face. Luckily, the pneumonia had cleared as the final equipment testing was being completed, and his first day back on the job coincided with the first day the factory was set to resume normal operation.

Beaming from his luck at having survived the pneumonia and avoided the maintenance, Wade walked back into the locker room. All he needed were a few safety pins to hold the slack in place, and he'd be ready to start the day. This temporary solution would be enough; he didn't plan on staying this weight. Rather than paying off medical bills, Wade intended to spend his next paycheck on regaining a sizeable chunk of his normal pudginess. He didn't feel like himself when he was this close to being thin.

The pins were stored in the sewing kit used to mend the uniforms, inside a metal cabinet next to the first aid station. Designed to be used on thick fabric like denim, the pins were thick and sharp and easily punctured his dense cotton coveralls. It took nine to hold down the fabric flaps around his legs, waist, and shoulders. Now able to swing his arms and move freely, Wade was satisfied that his attire conformed to the plant's safety standards and put the sewing kit back.

A whir of machinery unexpectedly hummed through the locker room, prompting Wade to slap on his protective earmuffs. He had thought he could get back to the floor before they switched the production line on, but missing the start-up routine was just a small disappointment. He double-checked the pins and left the locker room.

Jeff and the others were out of sight, and the conveyor was moving, unattended. No appliance parts came down the line, so Wade guessed it was still warming up. Everything seemed brand new and, like Wade, ready to go. The conveyor's freshly cleaned metal rollers shined back at Wade's positive appraisal. Guessing that

Jeff and the others were at the control station, Wade weaved toward the stairs, around the conveyor and its fabricator.

The large machine that measured, crimped, and cut power cords was running too. Its innards moved back and forth as Wade approached from behind, although no cords were being deposited into the basket beside it. As an entry-level assembler, this had been Wade's first station. He recalled the hours he had spent motivating himself by gazing at the main console above, just up the stairs nearby. His extra efforts had earned him recognition and a series of promotions. Now he worked quality control at that main console. Remembering how far he had come renewed his cheer.

Upon rounding the corner, Wade's cheer died. A young man standing next to the machine's input stood paralyzed, like a mannequin. His face was crumpled in terror and confusion. A chrome spirit, stretched into a spear, pierced the man's chest. Its arms wriggled outward. Its kicking legs protruded from the man's back. The spirit struggled, jerking as if its frayed, dangling clothes had snagged the man's ribs. Wade tried to decide what to do.

The specter spun to free itself, and as it did, the man twisted as well. His right arm bent toward the machinery fruitlessly crimping, measuring, and cutting nothing. Its steel feeding pincers nabbed the man's sleeve and dragged his arm down a short track. Programmed to measure a specific length, the cutters snipped off the excess portion of the man's hand. Wade's fascinated eyes followed the four fluttering fingers as they tumbled into the recycling bin, still connected by webs of skin.

The machinery had to be stopped—all of it. Wade didn't know what to do about ghosts, but he could prevent the equipment from injuring anyone else. His station had an emergency shutoff. He just needed to get to the main console. He turned his back on the ghost and its blood-spurting host and ran for the stairs, but halted the moment his foot touched the bottom step. At the top, three tangled spirits were fighting over Jeff's body. They blocked the only path up.

"Criminy!"

Jeff faced away from Wade. His right hand was locked around the railing while his left clawed at the air. If Jeff was screaming, Wade couldn't hear him through the earmuffs. One of the ghosts, a male, wore a cracked helmet and flailed at the others. A second male had the crazed expression of a desperate man who had found a golden egg. It reached into the socket where Jeff's left arm joined his shoulder and dug around inside. A third ghost, a small, bony woman, encircled Jeff's belly and seemed to be yelling at the males. None appeared to notice Wade, but he dared not advance.

The spirits continued fighting, snapping, and swinging at each other while Jeff's body spasmed in response. His legs bent outward, pulled in opposite directions by the paranormal brawl, and in mid-step, his legs faltered. Jeff fell stiffly backward, wrenching his right hand loose, and toppled sideways down the stairs. Time slowed for Wade as Jeff smashed his temple onto the railing, cracking open the thinnest part of his skull. The three spirits immediately stopped fighting, looked around, and disappeared.

Freed from their grasp, Jeff's body collapsed and flip-flopped down to Wade's feet. The new hire behind Wade lay silently on the floor too. Wade couldn't tell if his coworkers were dead or knocked out. Either way, he didn't have time to check for more casualties. He held his breath, hopped up the stairs, slammed the emergency shutoff, and raced back down. Exhaling shakily, Wade surveyed all directions. Nothing. No people and no ghosts. He sprinted back to the locker room to call an ambulance, then returned to dress the two injuries he knew about. Wade couldn't stop ghosts, but he might be able to stop the bleeding.

5

FRIDAY

NA'S BRUSQUE REENTRY into Zeb's office a few days later startled the middle-aged woman standing in front of the desk. Na's mouth, already open to speak, snapped shut, and then opened again to say, "I'm sorry, Dr. Elmir—?"

"Greetings, Na. Rojana Bensen, this is Dr. Shula, dean of Arts and Sciences. She's just granted me leave to conduct research in my field of expertise. Substitutes will take the reins of my courses, including a cultural anthropology adjunct for your Culture 209."

"Oh?" said Na, perplexed. She glanced down at the papers in her hand, translations of her family's conversations and Thai websites that reported on supernatural incidents, and remembered why she was there. "I brought some information for you. Do you still want it?"

"Absolutely. Dr. Shula, this is the student I'd like to bring with as my research assistant. Although she's only a sophomore, she has a personal interest in the subject and is both committed and determined."

Dr. Shula shook Na's hand. "Hello, Ms. Bensen. I think it would be great for Dr. Elmir to have an assistant this time. But understand that if you go with him, you'll have to drop the courses you are currently taking, which may affect your financial aid. You'd get paid, but it's not much since it's classified as an internship."

"Um, hello, Dr. Shula. I don't understand. What's going on?"

"Ghosts, Na. Ghosts, perhaps, are in Milton. I have a website where people share details of their sightings in exchange for answers to their questions. Mostly I get pranks, videos of people under sheets, etcetera, but this past Tuesday, I got one worth investigating. Three workers were killed and two were hospitalized in what was either an industrial accident or, as one witness is saying, a mass sighting.

"The witness is cogent. I've spoken with him, and I've verified the accident happened. Milton is only a couple days' drive from here, but since it'll take time to do interviews and put reports together, you would have to take this term off, and we need to leave right away. What do you think? If you'd like to take the internship, I believe Dr. Shula has the forms with her now for you to fill out."

Na had planned to scold Dr. Elmir for his criticism of Sompob's story, something she felt fully prepared to do with a bundle of evidence in her hands. But given the chance to find her own answers and get some peace of mind that could be shared with her family, Na checked her irritation for the moment. "Yes, I accept. I live with my parents, so leaving quickly isn't a problem."

"Glad to hear it," said Zeb, standing to shake Na's hand. "Here are copies of my correspondence with the witness, a man named Wade Havelock. His memories and those of the first responders won't stay fresh for long, so we should head out early Monday morning."

Na plopped her translations on Zeb's desk and accepted his packet. "Okay. I'll deliver the forms to Dr. Shula tonight, and I'll do the reading later. My number's there, for when you have details. It was nice meeting you, Dr. Shula." Na wordlessly departed as abruptly as she'd entered. She had many things to explain and a few things to pack before Monday.

6

MONDAY

"I CAN'T STRESS this enough, Na. You must stay off social media. No posting, no liking, no favoriting. I even recommend no reading. It's easier to resist the urge to reply if you don't know what's going on. You cannot leak any aspect of our plans to anybody. If you do, people will clam up, or worse, reporters and bloggers will start snooping."

"Sure, no problem."

"You'll be conducting qualitative interviews to get a feel for the town's local culture, especially to find out how receptive they are to the idea of ghosts. That will give us context and may tell us how commonly they report supernatural activity. I'll handle the witness interviews. Being able to talk to witnesses so soon after a mass sighting is rare, and I want to use an assessment of mine to gather the initial data."

"Sure." *The trees along the highway are a lot like the trees in Bangkok,* Na thought. From a distance, they were identical. They had the same mix of dark and bright greens, forming clusters that were both inviting and ominous. Only when the car drove right past them could she tell the plants here were different from those surrounding her cousins' homes. The shapes of the leaves and the curves of the branches were more varied, more flamboyant, in Thailand.

She tried to listen intently to Dr. Elmir, but he was skirting the issue. Tuning in to his monologue from time to time to nod politely and see if he'd gotten back on track—". . . I put the assessment together some years ago, hoping I'd be fortunate enough one day to . . ."—had been disappointing, so she appreciated the landscape instead, reining in her irritation.

Was he deliberately avoiding the possible connections between Sompob and Milton to keep her listening? The similarities were plain as day; they were right there in the emails from Wade and the translations from her family. Was he so clueless that he didn't understand why she had agreed to come?

She spotted a live alpaca for the first time in her life. But as soon as she noticed it, they had passed it, and as the alpaca faded into the distance behind them, so did her patience.

"Dr. Elmir, can we talk about what happened? The attack in Milton sounds like the attack on Sompob. That's two ghost attacks with witnesses in a short time, but you still don't think attacks are real, right? I need to know what happened. I need to know if it will happen again. I need to know my family will be okay."

"We don't know enough to say much yet," he answered immediately. "Let's leave that conversation until we're at the motel. I'll make some calls, let them know we're coming, get a few contacts, and then we can talk about it. I really doubt the two events are related, though. The world's a big place, and ghost stories are told everywhere. I read the articles and notes you gave me yesterday. We don't know all that much about the sighting in Milton right now, and I haven't heard anything that indicates the two are linked. We need to avoid falling for post hoc, ergo propter hoc. One event following another does not indicate the first event caused the second, nor does it mean they are related."

He's damned skeptical for a "true believer," Na thought, but she didn't have the will to object. The soft whistle of air around the car was lulling her to sleep, despite her vexation. The tires' hum joined in to carry her hazy mind away to the ocean, a far more serene place than this car with this old man. She did not resist. From drowsiness and resignation, she agreed to put the conversation on hold.

ZEB MADE SEVERAL calls before reaching a Milton official who accepted his credentials. It took using research terms like "methodical inquiry" and "informed consent," but Zeb finally learned the names and numbers of the doctor, local police, and city government personnel handling the situation. He knew where to start.

Through good manners and the proper channels, Zeb's great hope was to acquire the town's full cooperation, including access to formal reports. However, it was past five by the time the conversation ended, too late to call government offices. He circled CONTACT TOWN LEADERS, reread the last two items on the night's to-do list, and decided to call Wade before tackling the other.

"Good evening, Mr. Havelock. This is Zeb Elmir. I'm sorry I can't talk long. I expect to get into town late tomorrow. Are you still free the day after?"

"Dr. Elmir, you can't get here soon enough. I've got the whole day free, maybe the whole month free. They're saying I was negligent, that since I'm QC, this mess was my fault—that it's my fault Jeff . . . Yeah, get here when you can. I'm ready to talk to someone who wants to know what happened."

"Alright, I'll call tomorrow night to get directions and set a time. Until then, rest, relax, and keep making notes of any details you remember. I literally want to hear everything about it."

It wasn't easy to hang up, but Zeb couldn't get the data he needed over the phone. Wade appeared to be a good source, perhaps an invaluable one, and Zeb sympathized, too. He imagined himself sitting alone in an unguarded house, stewing, having just lost friends due to inexplicable tragedy. He closed his eyes and stroked his forehead. *What must wait must wait.*

Turning back to the list, he put a check next to WADE and retraced NA, thickening and darkening the letters. He understood her perspective; in fact, he counted on it to keep her moving without constant management. There had to be a way to work this out so she could put on her scholar hat without taking off her running shoes.

He didn't want to promise that helping in Milton would answer the concerns she had about Bangkok. Yes, she would walk away from the study with a greater understanding of life's facets, but aspects like the future security and well-being of her family were unknowable. All she or they could do was live day by day until whatever was going to happen happened, an axiom lost on the young.

Zeb looked out the large window ubiquitous in motels. While he'd been making calls inside his spacious, drab room, Na had been outside, setting up dinner on the small, round, plastic table meant to discourage people from smoking indoors. She had brought fried chicken, vegetable stir fry, and rice from her mother. Apparently, she had also hauled a chair out of her room so they could sit at the table together. The fried chicken drew him outside.

Pleasantly chilled from the cooler, the chicken's salty softness provided an easy way to break the ice. "This is good, Na. I mean, it's really good. Thank your mom for me."

"Mom loves to fry."

"Anyway, I know why you took this job. It's the same reason I offered it to you. Wanting to resolve Sompob's troubles is going to keep you interested and focused, even if the work gets tedious, which it probably will. But . . ."

Na stopped chewing.

". . . those feelings can be a problem, too. Take the interviews you'll be doing. Your body language and facial expression can change how people respond. They'll say what they think you want to hear, even if it's not really true, because most people would rather fib a little than risk hurting your feelings."

Na nodded and swallowed. "I know that. I took journalism in high school."

"Great. So if your feelings can have that strong of an effect while you're doing interviews, think about the effect they can have when you're sorting their responses to find recurring themes. If you decide the meaning of what people said before analyzing their words, your analysis will be incomplete at best."

Na broke eye contact to nab a drumstick from the Tupperware, which Zeb interpreted as a good sign.

"I know you want to talk about Sompob, but we can't, not yet. First impressions are hard to change, and our first impression of what happened has to come from what the witnesses say, not from any guesses we have right now."

"So, we will talk, but not until later," she paraphrased, covering her mouth as she spoke.

"Right. We're dealing with a subject that most people are incredulous about, so it's doubly important for our research to be as pure as possible."

"In other words, I need to be patient."

"Right."

"You could have just said that."

"Right. Do you have more chicken?"

8

NA SAT ON her motel bed, surrounded by sheets of interview questions and annotated articles from Dr. Elmir. With one more day's drive ahead before reaching Milton, she needed to study and prepare. But she could still taste her mom's veggie stir fry, and since coming to her room, she'd found it hard to concentrate.

Her mother had been displeased by her decision to go alone on a trip with a man, but for Sompob and the extended family, the mutually recognized objections about impropriety had gone unsaid. Na was glad for that; a conversation about appearances would have forced Na to voice her increasingly negative feelings about Dr. Elmir, and knowing those feelings would have just made her mother worry more.

Na had worried about the trip too—because of her duties and the possibility of being supernaturally assaulted like Sompob. Tonight, however, as she read and practiced asking questions, the inner calm that came from following organized procedure soothed her mind. It was the most relaxed she had felt in weeks. Constructive tasks replaced nagging troubles, and she was happy she was here. She missed her mom, a distraction that nabbed her attention every time she licked her teeth, but hoped that being here would help the entire Bensen/Suetrong family. Her only residual concern was how much trust and faith she could put in Dr. Elmir.

Around campus, students said that Dr. Elmir was a passionate proponent of the otherworldly, which meant his courses were a lot of work and a little freaky. During that first meeting in his office, though, he had been thickheaded and cynical. He had made no attempt to grasp the depth of the trauma her family was experiencing.

"It wanted to *kill me*," Sompob had told her. The enmity of the ghost distressed and confounded Sompob. From him, the shock of the assault had rippled throughout Na's family. Suspicious questions followed in its wake. Why Sompob? Each member clung to a different answer. His father believed that the ghost had been sent by an enemy, possibly a neighbor, and it would come again. Others suggested that ghosts could get lost just like people did, or that it had mistaken Sompob for someone else. An uncle had been heard mumbling, "Maybe Sompob's not as clean as we think he is." The uncertainty was damaging her family's unity. Doubt was the only feeling everyone shared.

Dr. Elmir's doubt was on a whole different level. He had boldly stated that the report, as Sompob gave it, was impossible. He had said the trauma consuming Na's thoughts, dominating her dreams, and rattling her family did not happen. Yet he had given Na the chance to come with him to Milton, to find out what had happened there. In gratitude, she resolved to acknowledge any good deed he did, to give him the chance to counterbalance that one big negative: his doubt.

Tonight, Dr. Elmir had earned a measure of credit. He had hinted at having the frankness and faith Na desired to see. He could be forthcoming when he wanted to be. What he'd said about giving interviews was true, too. So, dislodging the last string of celery from between her molars, Na refocused on the work at hand.

She meticulously studied Zeb's notes, articles, and questionnaires well into the night, knowing she could nap in the car tomorrow. Gradually, the dryness of his writing style eased Na into sleep. As she clicked off the light, her drowsy thoughts lingered on her family and the nature of ghosts rather than Dr. Elmir's obstinacy.

Na lay in comfortable slumber until a soft breeze on her calves sent shivers up her legs, jolting her awake. A lump of air caught in her throat at the sharp change in breathing, and she coughed loudly and put her hands over her mouth to stifle the sound. No movement was audible through the wall; she hadn't disturbed Dr. Elmir next door. She swallowed to moisten her throat, and her eyes wandered the room inquisitively. The door was locked, and the window was closed. Her legs felt warm and toasty under the covers, but there had definitely been a breeze. She still felt the cold of it. Had someone walked past the bed?

The bathroom next to the entry was the darkest part of the room. The bathroom door hung halfway closed, and Na couldn't see inside. Her back tightened as she slowly rolled to her feet. There were no weapons to brandish, not even metal silverware. Steadfast, she curled her fingers, took a step, leaned forward, and shoved the bathroom door open. It bashed against the doorstop and shook on its hinges. Na switched on the light and saw nothing. No one was inside.

Certain in her security and aloneness, she left the bathroom light on and returned to bed. A full, fitful hour of phantom tickles passed before Na successfully coaxed herself back to sleep. As she slept, her agitated mind wrestled with images of demons tormenting her family, searching for her.

PART 2

MILTON

9

TUESDAY

ZEB AWOKE AT 6:18 Tuesday morning and was instantly disappointed to find himself still at the motel. He had driven to Milton in at least three separate dreams. He scratched his back, dismissed the tiny motel coffee maker, and prepared for the actual drive, beginning by piling everything he'd unpacked in the center of the bed.

His field, paranormal anthropology, wasn't a crowded one. He wasn't racing to beat fellow researchers. Zebediah's enthusiasm was purely about the data. The chance to get data so pure, collected so close to the event, thrilled him, which increased his odds of forgetting something.

He double-checked the drawers and shelves, even those he knew he hadn't used. The bottom shelves of the nightstands, inconvenient and forsaken by the housekeepers, coated his hands in dust. Slapping the sides of his pants, he glanced around one more time. It was better to be safe than to risk leaving a page of notes behind. *Will Na be as thorough?* He would ask to make sure.

Over time, people could replace what they actually saw with what they expected to see and eventually with what they wanted to see. That was as true of packing as it was of witnessing hauntings. Most tales of manifestations were embedded in local cultures. They evolved and gained embellishment years after the events that inspired them: "To see the Walking People, face backward and go slowly down this path, past these graves, between 1 and 2 AM when the moon is full and covered by clouds . . ." Separating original versions from the add-ons became impossible. People even confused snippets of overheard phrases with what they saw themselves.

This one special time, there would be less of that nonsense to sort through. He would be among the first to talk to witnesses, visit the site, and collate reports.

Okay, maybe his excitement wasn't purely about the data. Maybe it was also a chance for verification, or better yet, vindication. His ideas about the afterlife were thoughtful and developed, but they were technically more like beliefs than hypotheses. A requirement of any good hypothesis was testability, which was hard to come by in his field. However, with firm data, he might finally acquire solid evidence that could be spoon-fed to skeptics and cynics. *If ghosts really* were *involved.*

But he had confidence. Wade's account was unique and highly unlikely to be a mere industrial accident. *That many injuries among that many people who work within safety protocols and designated stations? No, not without a stimulus to set things in motion, something that could be present one instant and gone the next without a trace.*

It was time to shower. Zeb swiveled the showerhead and let the water's heat mellow his jubilation. Even if everything dead-ended in Milton, he might document the birth of a new local legend. With repeated visits, he could track the tale's development to see what the modern mythos created. It would be an interesting case study. If the nuggets of truth didn't support his hypotheses, they'd at least send him in new, more correct directions. Progress was guaranteed.

"Ghosts are real," he proclaimed, "and I will know why." Goose bumps rose along his forearms. He luxuriated in the promise of validation.

Zeb made a final mental note. To avoid being added to the story as a Van Helsing character, he had to be unobtrusive. He couldn't be secretive or mysterious. He needed to join the town and observe as a bureaucratic visitor. *Yes, that's it,* he decided; he would identify himself as a researcher examining the "industrial accident," checking for similar events in the past and interviewing witnesses to get detailed accounts.

Na must be unobtrusive too, he thought. In her interviews, she had to stress that she was gathering local history, including fables of town scandals and terrors. Given Na's mindset, a script would be necessary, with directions to follow the script to the letter. As he had warned her, she could corrupt the study by just hinting at her connection to the supernatural. *I cannot allow that.* Drying off with the hotel towel despite his better judgment, he finished packing while outlining the lecture he'd deliver to Na during the remainder of their drive to Milton.

10

NA SQUEEZED THE back of her neck. The muscles supporting her skull twinged from nodding repetitively to Zeb's spiel. Yes, be direct; yes, be unbiased; yes, be controlled; yes, be unassuming; yes, be polite; yes, be focused; yes, be serious; yes, be simple. The verse on simplicity was gratuitously similar to the verse on directness.

Na had woken up with renewed appreciation for her role as Dr. Elmir's assistant. They welcomed each other in the morning with warm smiles and shared anticipation, but since the car doors had closed, the only break from his overbearing tone had come from a granola bar's raucous crunch. Twisting her shoulders to stretch, she regarded his profile. As taxing as his lecture was, she understood where it came from. He was excited and didn't want her to screw everything up. She squeezed her neck again and kept listening as best she could.

Some rambling verses later, they passed an ash with broadly outstretched branches, and a large sign came into view: MILTON! WE'RE BRINGING POWER TO FULTON'S PEOPLE! A picture of a power station surrounded by trees filled the space beneath, revealing nothing about the power's source. *They need a new slogan,* Na thought. She halfheartedly imagined alternatives:

> *Your Plain Ticket!*
> *No one ever came from here.*
> *Who wants to be a Miltonaire?*
> *We're haunted!*

"Here it is," said Dr. Elmir. They coasted down a gently curving off-ramp, which weaved through woods, and the town came into view. Milton appeared flat, undeveloped, and deserted. There were cars here and there, a few structures, and hardly any people. The off-ramp merged onto an arterial: Hansen Road. Immediately afterward, they pulled over and parked in front of a four-story brick building. "And this is where we're staying. That was easy."

Na read the name aloud: "The New Mill Hotel."

"Yep. It doesn't seem very new."

Na returned his dumb grin with a half smile. "Maybe the mill was new."

"Let's go find out." He eagerly bounded out of the car.

Na moved more slowly. She opened the door, put her feet on the ground, and reached, touching her toes. Yawning, she stood and looked around. Dr. Elmir was already inside the lobby, the hotel's door closing slowly behind him. The orange-red building stood solidly. Its age showed in a rectangle of paint blotches speckling a windowless section near the roof. Whatever used to be advertised there was indecipherable now. Na cynically figured it had hawked mummy dust, rhino horn, or tinctures of other powdered mammal parts.

A small store neighbored the hotel. Built in strip-mall style, it was short, flat, and gray with cheap beige trim. The storefront window read STUFFS in hand lettering. Carefully displayed candy boxes included a row for Kokomyntz. Na spotted an expanse of grass beyond the store, probably a park.

Turning, she spotted a defining feature of smaller towns: a single campus for three schools. Separate signs distinguished the grounds—MILTON ELEMENTARY, MILTON MIDDLE SCHOOL, and ROBERT FULTON HIGH SCHOOL: GO WILDCATS! The tranquil campus implied the school day hadn't ended yet.

It was all ordinary. Common. Dull. Nothing stood out. *Is this where we'll solve mysteries of the afterlife?* she wondered. *Where are the broken signs hanging off rusted chains? Or the dark, spiraling clouds? Where are the eccentrics, the miserable people in old, washed-out clothes shouting vague warnings of imminent doom? Perhaps the innkeeper is a crazy woman with a mutated appendage drooping from her chin.*

Na meandered into the hotel, wishing for the best. Or worst.

11

INSIDE THE SPACIOUS lobby, Na joined Dr. Elmir at the front desk, where he was being helped by a middle-aged woman with curled, brownish-blond hair. She typed on a laptop connected to an all-in-one printer/copier/scanner/fax machine as Dr. Elmir gave his registration information. Na couldn't find any backwater objects common to horror movie hotels. Rusted mechanical cash registers, fountain pens, and menacingly pointed receipt spindles were all conspicuously absent.

"We're never full these days, and this place is our home, so we like to give it a bed-and-breakfast feel," the woman was saying. "Meals are extra, and we need advance notice. We cook breakfast and dinner, and lunch is leftovers. If you're hungry now, I could make a couple roast beef sandwiches."

Dr. Elmir glanced at Na and said, "Sounds great. Hold the horseradish—"

"Don't on mine," she interjected.

"—and put us down for breakfast and dinner. We should be keeping regular hours."

"Meals . . ." The woman quickly entered a notation. "As requested, Mr. Elmir, you're in room 215. Ms. Bensen, you're in 315. My husband's out right now. Do you mind if we leave your bags here until he gets back?"

"Don't worry about it; we can get them," Zeb stated confidently.

Na didn't mind carrying her own bags. Although petite, she could easily heft her luggage thanks to years of playing softball. Sandwiches and room keys in hand, they hoisted their belongings up the stairs to avoid the "mischievous" elevator, as the woman had called it.

Na's bags were newish and came from a dark-blue polyester set her family had purchased four years ago. The three bags showed many signs of wear, ranging from tattered fabric to short, black lines of machinery grease and wonky wheels. Her parents' international flights had been rough on them. Dr. Elmir's bags, on the other hand, were strikingly pristine. The satchel for his laptop and papers was obviously brand new, and the hard, brown shells of his large case and matching carry-on, while downright archaic, had no scratches or cracks. Na inferred that Dr. Elmir either didn't travel much or mostly traveled by car.

"My room is beneath yours. We'll have privacy, but we're close enough to hear each other scream." He looked expectantly at Na, who could only manage a smile. Either the town's normalcy or the lecture had drained her of the energy needed to force a chuckle.

"Let's take it easy, settle in. We can meet at seven for dinner."

Na continued up without responding. Fourteen steps later, she reached the third-floor hallway. Small fixtures along the beige walls lit the hall dimly. The carpet, a sad olive green with gold lines in a grid pattern, wasn't especially worn.

"Three fifteen," she muttered. It was about halfway down. The key turned the loose knob freely, and Na pressed the door open with her shoulder. The room exhaled as if it had been holding its breath and swept hair into Na's eyes. It was smaller than the motel room from the night before. The decor matched the earth tones in the hallway. A double bed, a nightstand, a small table with a chair and a chest of drawers with a TV on it filled the space. Two woodsy pictures hung above the bed. One depicted a couple strolling through trees, and the other showed people fly-fishing in a river. A tiny refrigerator stood in the corner, waiting to be plugged in. She dropped her bags and collapsed onto the bed. Everything felt dry and crispy, even the comforter. The room, the entire floor, was silent and calm. Na was not.

I wanted to be here, right? I wanted to stay in a bland hotel in a mundane town, where everything, including the sandwiches, is boring.

Despite a palpable purpose, discontentment overtook her. She told herself to relax; they had only just arrived. She should reserve judgment. To break the mood, she proclaimed, "It's not so bad. It could be worse. It'll have to do." Her words sank in. This place *would* have to do. She needed a walk.

It was exceedingly refreshing to retreat down the stairs, through the lobby, and out the main double doors. Transitioning from afternoon to evening, the still-bright sun lit up the world with colors that went unrepresented inside the dreary hotel. Brilliant green grass, azure sky, chromium-silver car details, and chalk-white street paint glowed all around. Best of all, Stuffs remained open.

Chimes jingled as she entered. "Hello!" an obviously energetic young man called from the rear of the efficiently organized store. "What can—"

"Kokomyntz?" Na asked, cutting him off.

"Sure, they're over here. Those boxes in front are for display," the man clarified. "It was fun emptying them."

"You've made my day," Na mumbled.

"Not having a good trip?"

Na paused to scrutinize him.

"Uh, I saw you go into the hotel. What do you think of the place?"

The lean, plainly dressed cashier couldn't have been more than a year or two older than her, putting his age at twenty-one at most. His short, umber hair hinted he was too busy to be fussy. Relaxing, she approached him at the register. A sizeable array of assorted individual candy bars occupied the area.

"It's okay."

"When I graduated last year, we had a big party there. I think that was the loudest it's been in years. So, how is your trip? Will you be staying long?"

"It's too soon to tell. I'm not sure how long we'll be."

"Well, there's not much to see. We're just Milton—just kind of here, doing our thing. What brings you?"

Na stooped to eyeball the "king-size" boxes, which seemed smaller than she remembered. "Checking out the town, its history. I'm helping with a study."

"Ah, local history. Mills and the decline of the working class and stuff like that?"

"Sort of."

"Then you should visit the museum. It's down the main street a ways, on the other side of City Hall. It's got a little of everything, from the first settlers to local wildlife. However, if you want to hear a story, I'm the man to see. Born and raised here, I know them all."

Intrigued, Na straightened to meet the cashier's gaze and challenged, "You know them all?"

"Sure do. I'm Doug, by the way." He lifted his forearm, and Na thought he was going to go for a handshake, but he made a fist and rapped the counter with his knuckles instead.

"So you know about the family that runs the hotel? Why this street's named Hansen Road? Who the mayor hates the most?"

"Yep, yep, and yep!" he exclaimed.

Zeb's plea for patience, still present in her head, couldn't fend off the temptation. "Alright then. Tell me a ghost story."

"A ghost story?"

She nodded.

He broke eye contact for a moment. "Yeah. Yeah, I've got one." He swallowed and lowered his voice. "Ninety years ago, we had a dentist here in Milton who didn't approve of numbing his patients. No anesthesia, period."

"Ouch."

"Yeah. He was working on a lumberjack who had a huge, black cavity on one of his front teeth. The dentist drilled away, filling the air with that smell of burning bone. In those days, drills were powered by foot pedals, you know. Anyway, big, tough, and fearless, the lumberjack sat like a statue, taking it without a wince. The dentist stopped for a second to make sure the guy was fine. He gave a thumbs-up, so the dentist leaned over and resumed drilling. Suddenly, he hit a nerve dead-on. In reflex, the lumberjack swung his giant hand and smacked the dentist's head, knocking him off balance. The dentist's arm slipped, and the sharp drill tore the lumberjack's throat open like a knife through a sail in a pirate movie."

"Thanks for the imagery."

"No problem." He winked. "The lumberjack didn't have any family nearby, so it was called an accident, and they buried him somewhere. That was the dentist's last patient. He quit. Even though his office was only a few yards behind his house, he never returned to it. The house collapsed long ago, but the rotting office is still there on Taylor Street. You can still get inside, and if you do, you might see the lumberjack. My friends have seen him. They say if you go there at night and step on his dried blood, he'll appear and come at you, swinging his fists wildly like you're the one who killed him.

"How's that for a ghost story?"

"Not bad," Na admitted. She dropped a handful coins on the counter and opened the candy she'd selected.

"It's true, too." Doug winked again. "I've got more. Come back whenever you're ready for another."

Sucking on Kokomyntz and armed with a lead, Na felt better about Milton and its hotel. Room 315 seemed bright and welcoming when she reentered. The crispy bed felt clean rather than stiff and starchy. Even the sandwich from the front desk smacked of edibility. Finally, Na decompressed. She could eat.

Munchies satiated several minutes later, she fell asleep next to an empty box of candy and a ball of plastic wrap twisted into the shape of a cat's head.

12

ZEB LOVED THE hotel. The air of the snug room, its enveloping peacefulness, mimicked his office. He definitely belonged here. He used every clean drawer and shelf as he unpacked, placing each item in its predestined location. With a quick phone call, he scheduled Wade's interview for tomorrow morning. His to-do list still had CONTACT TOWN LEADERS circled. He chose to postpone that one more day. The more he knew about what had happened, he reasoned, the more convincing his rationale would be for garnering access to their reports. Organized and settled, he took a break to eat his deliciously mild horseradish-less sandwich.

Fully satisfied, he got to work. Zeb reread his notes start to finish, tweaked his interview questions, and then turned his attention to Na's duties. Word by word, he scripted Na's introduction and queries. The initial information he wanted her to gather about the town's setting and population wasn't delicate. Her performance on that first task would determine how quickly he trusted her with more difficult tasks. She was obviously astute, which made Zeb hopeful, but she lacked control. Putting it in *X-Files* terms, he would play the deliberate, rational Scully to her reckless Mulder.

And now, at 7:10 PM, he needed to be Na's clock. The phone rang six times before Na answered. "Mmm-nyello?"

"Have a good nap?"

"Wha? Yeah. Oh, Dr. . . . yeah."

Apparently, it had been a very good nap. "Let's meet downstairs. They said we can use their 'business center,' a locked room with a computer, printer, and a couple tables. You'll see it in the lobby."

"I'mcomingdown," she slurred back.

Mere seconds later, Zeb was set up and waiting in the stuffy, austere business center. A full fifteen minutes after that, he heard Na's knock and caught the second half of the world's biggest yawn. She held up a sandwich. "Sorry, I went to get another one. Hungry."

"You don't mind eating dinner here? I got the innkeeper's permission. We don't want others to overhear our plans."

"Nope."

"Great." Na sauntered inside as Zeb darted out. His mind racing over tomorrow's schedule, he picked up his dinner tray and returned, barely conscious of the meal's description: chunky tuna casserole and corn chips.

Zeb handed a glass of water to Na, who had sat at the empty table. He raised his own glass. "Cheers. Let's get started."

Na nodded politely and took a bite of her sandwich as he dug into the casserole. "How's dinner?" she asked.

"Thick." He drained half his glass, took another large bite, and handed Na the script he had composed. "You'll need this for tomorrow. It lists the data you'll collect first."

"We're not meeting Wade?"

"We'll split up to save time. While I interview Wade, you'll capture the local ambience to supplement its demographics. It will be your first day working officially as a research assistant. I have confidence in you."

She scanned the pages quietly.

"That's a script I want you to follow. To compare respondents' answers, you need to ask the same questions in the same order, using the same wording and intonation each time. Read it out loud tonight to get a feel for it."

"Okay." She struggled before speaking again. "I think I have a lead."

Zeb gulped down a partially chewed mouthful of gooey noodles. "A lead?"

"I know where a ghost might be."

"Do tell."

She leaned forward, putting an elbow on the table and gesturing with her hands. "There's an abandoned dentist office. A man died there years ago. At night, you can make him appear."

Zeb steadied himself. "Who told you this?"

"Doug, next door at Stuffs. He's talkative and offered to tell a story."

"What do you think we should do with this information?"

"We should investigate. If the ghosts came from there, we can warn people and get them to tear it down."

Zeb sighed loudly. "Like I've said, Na, there are rules we need to follow. Let me be explicit. The undead do not come up in everyday conversation. People don't say, 'Hey, how are you doing? I think my cat's a vampire.' Do not mention the afterlife or the undead to anyone at all unless I specifically ask you to."

"Well, we were talking, and—"

"And if someone tries to talk to you about anything undead related, avoid it. End the conversation if you have to. We don't want others' biases coloring our views any more than we want our own biases to color the witnesses' views. Either way, my study, the reason we're here, could be put in jeopardy."

"Got it. No ghosts, no undead anything. I'll wall it out." She exaggeratedly mimed in the air.

Zeb ignored the physical sarcasm. "As for the dentist office, yes, it might be worth investigating sometime to get the context of the story, but it's clearly not factual. It's a tall tale, told to make somewhere that's already spooky seem spookier, a place where teenagers take dates. In other words, it *is* part of the town's culture, but it's not directly tied to the event at the plant."

"It might be real. There's a museum; they might have records," she pleaded. "Shouldn't we see?"

"Yes, and we will, but first things first. Every town has its own tales, and I've heard lots of them. Lots. In many ways, they're all the same. There's a tragic death, some form of injustice or abandonment, and then some way of compelling the 'ghost' to appear, as if spirits care what the weather is like or who's touching their stuff. Does your story have a tragic death?"

He waited.

"Yes . . ."

"An injustice or abandonment, a rejection of some sort?"

"Kind of."

"So, there you go. It's a tall tale. Going to an old dentist's office when it's dark— It is at night when this 'ghost' appears?"

"Yes, like I just said."

"It would be dangerous, at best. It's the epitome of what I said a minute ago. We can't have tall tales mixing with legitimate data."

"Aren't tall tales based in reality, like Paul Bunyan and Johnny Appleseed?"

"That's not the point."

Na wrapped up the remaining three-fourths of her sandwich. "I've got the point. Don't ask, don't tell, don't investigate. Thanks for the script. I'll follow it letter by letter. I'm full and tired, so I'll see you tomorrow at dinner, if that's okay." Without missing a beat, she sang, "Have a peaceful evening!" and left the business center, closing the door firmly.

Zeb plopped down his plate, indifferent to his fork sliding sideways into the casserole, and ran his hand through his hair. *Which is worse, her story or her temper?* he wondered rhetorically. She hadn't listened to him, and when he called her on it, she grew mad. He had planned what to say at every opportunity and precisely reminded her of previous conversations, emphasizing points that Na herself had already acknowledged. Nevertheless, she had stormed out. Would this gamble on hiring a sophomore work? Perhaps Na couldn't separate herself from her family's involvement, despite knowing the necessity of doing so.

He didn't quite understand her obsession. It was a cousin in another country who had been hurt, not a parent or sibling; but perhaps her family truly was that close—so much closer than his that he had underestimated her emotions.

It didn't matter. There was plenty to do, much of it tiresome. She could still be useful. This might even be better. He could wall her out completely—as she had mimed—to limit the damage she could cause, while dangling the promise of learning secrets in her face. Tomorrow he could say, "Fascinating chat with Wade today. I can't tell you about it yet. How did things go for you?" If she was bent on being directly involved, her yearning to know more might help contain her emotions, might force her to behave. Meanwhile, he could jump straight into the good stuff. It was a manipulative trick used by kindergarten teachers, but it was necessary, he told himself. After all, he had high expectations for this once-in-a-lifetime study.

He carried his things up to his room and set the alarm for tomorrow morning. Then, Zeb whittled the night away crunching on chips and detailing, reviewing, and revising his notes.

13

WADE LIVED OUTSIDE town on a winding, forking road that made tracking directionality impossible. Zeb slowed to read every character of its sparse street signs to ensure he was going the right way. Dense forest lined the road, with driveway after driveway snaking into the foliage. They all cried, "Keep out! Leave us alone!" which was the opposite of what he knew Wade to be feeling. Wade was more than ready to open up.

Zeb hadn't wasted a moment dwelling on Na before leaving for Wade's. She would either do her assignment or not, and as he pulled alongside a large, aluminum mailbox hand-painted with Havelock, she was far from his mind.

Wade's gravel driveway stretched back through the trees, abruptly terminating at a small brown house. The woods surrounded the structure but let enough light through to keep moss off the roof. Zeb parked in front of the small detached garage, got out, and checked the trees above for precarious branches. The weather forecast had not mentioned strong wind; his car should be safe.

A little distracted by his excitement and drifting thoughts, he looked back toward the house and jumped. A large, whiskered man in frayed, loose-fitting clothes was approaching quickly. Countless scenes from crime dramas flashed in Zeb's mind.

"Doctor Elmir?" At Zeb's hesitant nod, the man slowed his pace, smiled, and held out his hand. "I'm Wade. Good to see you." Before Zeb could react, Wade tottered and gripped the car's fender. "I'd love to take a walk, but these antidepressants have me dizzy as hell. Can we head inside?"

Zeb lifted the satchel with his laptop. "That's better for me."

"Good deal."

Wade didn't speak again until they reached the porch. "Take your shoes off, if you don't mind. I like to keep the outdoors outdoors."

Zeb's favorite argyles, which he had enthusiastically stretched over his toes that morning, felt embarrassingly out of place against Wade's sensible socks. Zeb chided himself for forgetting the importance of fitting in during fieldwork. People were more receptive to requests when they could relate to the requester.

Wade led the way inside to a set of wood-framed sofas and chairs surrounding a large glass coffee table. Some loose-leaf papers sat on top. "You asked me for notes. Here they are."

Zeb didn't take the papers right away. The home's interior was beautifully decorated. Natural paneling enclosed an open kitchen, dining, and living area. It was filled with correspondingly stained tables and chairs.

"It's nice, isn't it? I kept the house small so I could build it exactly as I wanted."

Zeb nodded and then got down to work. "I'd like to get your story first, and then we'll go through these notes to fill in anything that got left out. You have the whole day free?" He arranged his things on the coffee table.

"What else can I do? They won't let me work like this, and I don't blame them. The doc says it'll take a spell to find the perfect dose. Who knows how long that'll be. Technically, I'm not even supposed to drive."

Feeling a bit like a therapist, Zeb gestured to Wade's own couch. "In that case, have a seat, and we'll take it slow. I'll ask some basic questions first, and then you can tell me what happened that day. Like I said, after that, we'll go over your emails and notes to add anything missing. Sound good?"

"Sounds good." Wade moved gingerly and sat down.

As Zeb had expected, Wade told a tale as impossible as Na's. According to Wade, ghosts had killed his boss, Jeff, and seriously injured another man. More feasibly, the men panicked and clumsily hurt themselves in the factory's dangerous environment. Zeb felt for Wade and his obvious pain at losing a friend, but his sympathy was dulled. Once again, the public's irrational fear of the dead had triggered preventable casualties. Zeb had always figured such fear came from too many horror movies and not enough perspective. Perhaps this study would gain enough attention to allay that fear, if only temporarily.

The good news was that Wade's tale matched his emails closely. Zeb watched for consistency for the same reason police did. Consistency indicated truth. His tale might not be possible, but as far as Wade knew, it honestly described what had happened. Dividing facts from miseducated suppositions was Zeb's job. He was an academic centrifuge.

Zeb's scalp tingled. *Focus*, he reminded himself. *Stay even. Now's not the time for exhilaration. Listen, make sure he fully answers every question. Don't get ahead of yourself.* "What happened once the emergency crews arrived?"

"That's where things get fuzzy." Wade flexed his hands. "They injected me with something to calm me down, and then they put me on these meds. When my head cleared, no one would hear me out. That's when I looked online and found your website."

"Your message made my day. Most of what I get are hoaxes not even worth replying to. Anyway, when did you hear what happened to the others who were hurt, the two that were crushed?"

"After I first emailed you. I didn't get the full story until company reps talked to me. I think everyone was intentionally hiding it before then to keep me calm. I told the reps what I'd seen. They didn't believe me. They're doing an investigation now, probing my records for drug use. They're trying to blame me. Maybe they'll tie it to my pneumonia and say I came back too soon. I don't know."

Wade fidgeted and gazed at his hands. "I've worked there for years, so I knew old-timers like Jeff. The others were new. I hadn't even met those two yet, and that other guy, I saw that guy lose his hand. I still don't know his name. And then he's on the ground, and his blood's all over me—"

"Yes, they haven't released his name to protect his privacy. Speaking of which," Zeb said, hoping a segue would settle Wade down, "will you sign a release so I can get your medical records?"

"Why not? The company already has them. I won't have real privacy again for a while." Wade paused. "I know they saw me. The ghosts. Dr. Elmir, am I safe?"

Ah, human nature, worrying about improbable dangers like lightning strikes rather than threats in front of us. Zeb had a response prepared. "Yes. Spirits do not and cannot hunt people. Even if they were capable of it, it would be like trying to track and hunt one specific duck among all the other ducks in a flock. Do not worry. You are safe."

14

BOONE HALES GRUMBLED, "This is the one where the daughter wants to wear a mermaid dress, but her mom wants her to wear her grandmother's dress, and then she starts crying about how it's *her* wedding. I'm *sure* you've seen this episode because *I've* seen it."

"It's a best-of show. We've only seen some of it."

"Do we *need* to see *all* of it?"

"Shhh!"

He nagged, but Taryn knew her dad liked this series about melodramatic fiancées and their overwrought kin. He never asked her outright to stop and watch it later, despite it being recorded on their DVR. She was pretty sure he'd teared up during the episode when the bride's father cried upon seeing his daughter in the perfect alabaster gown. This series was vicarious entertainment for both of them; Taryn hadn't married yet.

"By the way, Dad."

"What?" He didn't turn away from the TV.

"I almost forgot, I got a call the day before yesterday. A researcher's coming to look into that accident at the plant. I told him about the museum, so he'll probably stop by soon."

"I'm ready whenever. It's quiet this time of year—no school trips, so any time's fine. How is that going, anyway?"

"What?"

"The investigation. Do they know what happened yet?"

"No, the final report isn't finished. Most likely it was all caused by one guy. They're triple-checking every detail to satisfy OSHA. Herbie wants the plant to reopen soon, which means making sure the report covers all the bases. He thinks if the plant doesn't reopen quickly, there's no chance he'll get reelected."

"He's right. Whenever something goes wrong around here, the mayor gets the blame. That's how Herbie got elected in the first place, remember? Everyone was mad at Shultz because we got three feet of snow on Christmas. Hmph," Boone grunted resentfully. "Hey, you'd look good in this one. It's sort of like what your mom wore, with pleats."

"I don't like pleats."

"What's wrong with pleats? I won't buy pants without pleats. Except jeans."

"He asked about previous accidents, so if you have records of any, you may want to pull them to save time."

"Who?"

"The researcher. He wants to see if there's a history of accidents here, in Milton. Have there been others?"

"At the plant? No, first since it's opened, I think. There were probably some during the mill days. I'll check the archives. None could have been too bad."

If you don't know about it, no one does, Taryn mused proudly. Between his historical knowledge and personal connections, her father usually knew more about what was going on than she did, even though she worked for the mayor. He sometimes sounded anxious to get her out of the house, especially since she'd passed her thirtieth birthday, but she valued their time together and wasn't in a rush to get married, or move out, or find a potential suitor in the first place.

"What about this one, Taryn? It's asymmetrically left-handed. That's a good dress for a Hale."

"When I eventually go dress shopping, handedness won't be among my criteria."

15

NA YAWNED WITHOUT covering her mouth and stretched her arms in the early-evening sunlight. A pickup truck passed her on the street. *People are rude, life is rude; who cares if anyone sees my uvula.* She yawned again.

She had slept in extravagantly after spending much of the previous night meandering the nearby school campus, contemplatively gazing up at stars she couldn't see from home. Upon waking, she hastily escaped the hotel's confinement. She needed to be out on Milton's sidewalks, near movement, to think clearly and plan. Forget the interviews and data collection; those could be done later. As Na saw it, her two duties for the day were to relax and get ready for midnight. Both required a measure of peaceful roaming far from Dr. Elmir's ego and the self-satisfied expression he'd be wearing after visiting his star witness.

Thankfully, Dr. Elmir's distaste for her investigative stance likely meant that he'd be relieved rather than nosy when she didn't show up for their dinner tonight. She could shop and plan in solitude. Indeed, the evening hours passed with no contact from her professor, and she steeled herself for the task ahead.

Vandals had kept away from the ruined estate, letting the dentist's fallen house and relatively intact office cabin decay naturally. Her destination stood behind and to the left of the house. In the bright afternoon, the house had bristled menacingly on its abandoned property, spines of broken wood poking the air like an urchin.

Nightfall now obscured the hazards. Na intended to approach from the left side of the yard and loop toward the cabin, staying safely away from the house in case she lost her bearings in the darkness.

At last. It was almost eleven and dark enough to be called the middle of the night. She had killed sufficient time. Nearly everything was already stowed in her backpack. In final preparation, she cleared her smartphone's history to free memory, confirmed its settings, and slid it into her pocket. Recording at the highest quality possible, it should capture the lumberjack well enough to prove that ghosts *could* be aggressive. If recording meant taking a risk, so be it. Infuriating as he could be, Dr. Elmir understood things she didn't. She needed him on her side.

And anyway, Sompob had survived his encounter, and he was caught by surprise. She wouldn't be. Holding up a trusty new flashlight purchased from a locally owned, sells-everything-plus-gifts-for-nearly-forgotten-birthdays pharmacy, Na crossed the vacant road to the lot she had watched for the better half of a day.

Matted, gnarled weeds covered what had been a lawn. She had to slog through; no trail was visible. She lifted her feet high and plunged them blindly into the deep grass ahead as if tramping through snow. The dry stalks bent into points as she walked, needling her pant legs and scratching her skin. The pricks conjured images of biting, stinging creatures crawling underneath her clothes. If her foot struck a nest of rats or spiders . . .

She fought off the visions and continued marching.

Many stars twinkled above, but the world was dark. The crescent moon supplied little to no luminescence. Indistinguishable silhouettes surrounded her. She began to question the wisdom of tracing the left side of the yard for the sake of avoiding the depressed house. The yard bordered new-growth woods, which could be hiding anything: a rabid buck, wild dogs, tall men in heavy rubber gear. Na slowed her pace and listened between the loud mashing of her own steps. An intermittent breeze stirred the weeds like breathing. She suddenly realized the oddness of hoping to be alone while venturing toward a haunted cabin. There might be safety in numbers, but at the moment, one felt safer than three or four.

The cabin waited. Its entrance faced the woods, possibly for privacy or better natural lighting. Glass remaining in the shattered front window glinted in the flashlight's soft beam. Na veered toward it, leaving the uncertainty of the woods behind. She saw a patch of flattened weeds by the door, likely where drunk teenagers paused to debate the wisdom of entering a derelict building.

Upon reaching the patch, she chose to do the same and cautiously surveyed the cabin. Built of hewn logs, it was just large enough for two or three small rooms. The entrance was open and unobstructed. The door itself, missing its knob, lay on the ground across the threshold. Between the broken door and shattered window, nature had free access to the cabin's interior. Hidden nests of creatures sprang back to Na's mind.

"Hello?" she called out shyly. Na listened and shined the flashlight around. As before, she heard only rustling from the breeze—no scurrying. Satisfied she could proceed safely, Na stepped inside.

The first room was tiny and empty. It could have held three chairs and probably served as the reception area. Dried leaf skeletons, bits of wood, and other debris littered the gray floor. Many of the boards were cracked. Standing on the fallen door, she put one foot on the floor, testing her weight. The boards didn't give. She stepped off into the center of the room and looked up. Three absent roof planks allowed a partial view of the sky.

Webbing with desiccated insect husks filled every joint and corner of the interlocking logs that made up the walls. The exam room, Na's goal, had to be through the narrow doorway to her left. Na imagined patients sitting here ninety years ago, listening to others gagging and gurgling before it was their turn. There wouldn't have been whirs from air-conditioning or sleepy background music to mellow the mood.

In contrast to the empty reception area, the large exam room was a mess. It was about six meters long, five meters wide, and metal utensils were everywhere, reflecting the flashlight's beam into the shadows. Scattered trays and bowls and toppled shelving blocked Na's progress. Smaller instruments, mostly ancient dentistry tools, cluttered the room as well. Na found probes, scrapers, forceps, and saws, all with twisted prongs. Her stomach squirmed. Not for an instant did she consider picking one up.

What remained of the examination chair stood in the center of the room. A pedestal affixed to the floor propped up its frame. It looked less like a recliner and more like an adult-sized high chair, with wooden panels attached to cast iron. Some of the panels had molded and rotted, exposing metal bolts. She couldn't imagine herself sitting in it voluntarily, now or a hundred years ago.

According to the story, the bloodstain had to be near the chair, which was encircled by metal junk. Rather than raising a clamor by shoving the shelving, Na chose to disturb the scene as little as possible. The shelving forced her to sidle to her right. She carefully brushed instruments aside with her foot to avoid clanging them against one another. Passing an intact window, she shined her flashlight outward. She couldn't see much. Sticker bushes had grown up that side of the cabin, completely blocking her view.

Rounding the toppled shelving and nearing the chair, Na discovered the dental drill. It too had been knocked over. Its likely history of agony, coupled with the surrounding darkness, gave her a primal reaction. Her stomach squirmed again. The drill comprised a simple foot pedal with a wheel and wires for spinning the drill. Its wires had broken, and the actual drill, the part used on patients, was missing. Looking more closely, she saw the wheel was bent as if someone had stomped on it. Na realized it could have been the guilt-ridden dentist himself who had trashed the room and destroyed the drill. She couldn't fathom his level of despair, and she hoped she never would.

Standing next to the chair now, she visually explored the vicinity. *Where are you hiding?* Junk covered the floor on this side of the room too. Na feared that attempting to move things around would accidentally summon the lumberjack. Most of the floor was the same old gray color as the rest of the cabin. Discolored wood surrounded the chair's base, but the rusty hue seemed to come from the chair itself.

It occurred to Na that she didn't know how large of a stain to look for. The story was unclear. Should she search for a pool or spattered droplets? Perhaps most of the blood had dripped down the man's body, onto the chair, and then onto the floor. On second thought, he probably grabbed his neck, sat up, and fell forward as he died. His blood, then, the stain, would be in front of the seat.

Na assumed the bloodstain would be dark brown, but "brown" didn't have the narrative impact she wanted. According to Wikipedia, the color of dried blood, the color of lifelessness, was carmine. "I'm stepping on the carmine stain" sounded much more dramatic.

There. There, a faded splotch, the curve of a pool's edge, expanded out from under a large steel tray. That had to be the stain. Just enough was showing to step on it without removing the tray.

Na wasn't ready yet. She surveyed the room again to plan the quickest route out. Once the lumberjack appeared, he would likely come at her. Na needed enough space to dodge his lunge and get away, or she could end up worse than Sompob. She was alone; there were no neighbors nearby to investigate any shrieks or loud thumps she might make while in the lumberjack's grasp.

In front of her was the stain, then the metal shelving, and then the doorway she had come from. Behind her, a windowless wall held cupboards hanging over a counter with a built-in sink. The sink's drainpipe led straight down into the ground beneath. Its simplicity caught her attention. The pipe didn't have a trap. She guessed it emptied directly onto the dirt below, creating a muddy, gooey mix of mold, spit, plaque, and bits of teeth blackened from decay.

"Moving on," she mumbled. That wall joined with the shorter wall, also windowless, which in turn joined the wall with the intact window obstructed by stickers. The only easy way out was the path she had followed in. "Okay."

She reviewed her plan. She would start recording, step on the stain, wait, then run back around the shelves and out the door. It wasn't the quickest route, but she had already cleared the path, so there was no danger of tripping. She simply had to stay calm. "One swing," she said. "Capture one swing and run. Don't run too soon, don't run too late, don't panic."

Clearing her throat to shake any nervousness from her voice, Na lifted her cell phone and flashlight and began recording, sweeping the room as she narrated. "I'm in the dentist's office. There are cupboards lining the walls, and in the center is the chair where a man, a lumberjack, died. Here, on the floor in front of me, you can see his blood. I'm going to summon him now. I'm stepping on the carmine stain . . ."

Anticipation sensitized every nerve in Na's skin. At once, she felt the weight of the backpack on her shoulders, the seam of her socks along her toes, tangled lashes in the corners of her eyes, and the constriction of her bra across her chest.

Silence.

Where is he? Something swirled her hair gently, blowing a few strands into her eyelashes. She spun and took a step backward, catching the metal tray's edge and sending it clanging against the floor like a cymbal. Standing on the dead man's blood, she spun again, and back again, guarding both sides.

As she twisted on the spot, turning back and forth, she ground into a crack between the aged boards; the wood split, and her small foot plunged through. She gasped and immediately pulled up with all her strength, splintering the boards, freeing herself, and losing her balance. She stumbled back and slipped on the tray, flailing her arms and tossing her phone as she fell. Metal crashed like thunder as she tumbled onto the shelving, snapping a thin support bar under her weight. The bar's sharp tip slid into her upper right arm, piercing her triceps all the way through.

Dazed and numb from the fall, Na felt something wet on her skin and checked her arm with the light. She screamed at the metal goring her flesh and, without thinking, roughly pulled her arm free.

There was a lot of blood pouring out. She needed help. Na concentrated to gather her thoughts. *I need my phone.*

The glowing screen revealed its location at the base of the wall near the door. She climbed out of the wreckage noisily, picked up her phone, and pocketed it. She stumbled out into the night, holding the flashlight in her right hand and squeezing the now throbbing wound with her left. She didn't feel well. This wasn't just a cut. *So thirsty. Have to get to the road.* She lost strength with each stamp back through the tangled weeds. The land grew darker and colder.

Reaching the road at last, Na called 911. Maybe. She wasn't sure. Everything fogged. It was hard to think. The flashlight's bright glare hurt her eyes. She turned the light off and plopped down on the ground, gripping her bleeding arm as tightly as she could.

16

THE RECEPTIONIST HAD brought issues of *People*, *Arthritis Today*, and *Sunset* to Zeb upon his arrival, but they were still resting on the chair next to him, untouched. Wary of contagions, Zeb never handled magazines in doctors' offices. Instead, he went over his handwritten notes for the tenth time, going over every name, phone number, and conversation more from memory than the ink on the pages. The names of the doctor, factory rep, and sheriff had the same two words jotted next to them: UNDERSTANDABLY STANDOFFISH. While Na had apparently been injuring herself, he had obtained permission to move forward with his study. He retraced TOUR THE PLANT and couldn't help feeling a little excited.

A woman's soft voice roused Zeb. "Good, she's sleeping. I'll come back."

He promptly called after her in his loudest half whisper. "Nurse! Excuse me, Nurse."

The woman reappeared in the doorway. "Gina. How may I help you?" Nimble and wearing springy jogging shoes, she soundlessly entered the room.

"It's already ten. Is it normal to sleep this long from an arm injury?"

Continuing to speak softly, Gina addressed Zeb's anxiety. "The wound in Rojana's arm was the only injury we found. It will take some time to heal, and she'll need to wear a sling until it closes completely. Late last night, at the time she was admitted, she was in the early stages of shock. She is in no danger now, but her body is exhausted from the experience. She will most likely sleep through the rest of the day. Depending on how she is when she wakes up, she will be released tomorrow or the day after."

At first debating how much to reveal through his questions, Gina's perfect posture, gentle tone, and formal grammar fostered Zeb's trust. He smiled and replied, "That's comforting. Thank you. Do you have a minute for a few more questions?"

"Hm. Yes."

"There was an industrial accident a few weeks ago. Were you on duty then?"

"Yes."

"Did you treat Wade Havelock?" Showing her a paper, he added, "He signed a medical release. I'm trying to help him identify what he experienced; his memories from that day are muddled. He doesn't even remember what his initial statements were."

The nurse nodded. "Ah. Yes."

"And?"

Gina glanced at Na, who slumbered motionlessly, then replied in an even staccato, barely pausing to breathe. "When he arrived, Mr. Havelock was hallucinating, possibly from panic. Unlike your friend here, he had no injuries that could induce hallucinations. The paramedics had given him a sedative to calm his nerves, so by the time I saw him, he was not enunciating clearly. However, the paramedics said he had shouted warnings such as 'Watch out' and 'Don't go in there.'

"It is unclear if his hallucinations led to the accident or if the accident triggered panic and thus the hallucinations. We are treating the symptoms to make him more comfortable and increase his chances of a full recovery. In the short term, he'll need therapy to deal with what happened. The guilt from being involved in the deaths of three coworkers and the amputation of another's hand will surely weigh on him.

"Additionally, as you are probably already aware, his mental and physical states were delicate before the accident. He is still recovering from a severe bout of pneumonia, during which he also faced depression. Depression is common in those who endure long illnesses, especially those who live alone. Our goal now, as it was then, is to keep him calm and help him avoid stress. Stress and depression can make him vulnerable to a relapse of pneumonia and other opportunistic illnesses."

"Give me a moment, please, to get all of that down . . . Okay. Wade mentioned he was tested for drug use. What were the results?"

"Nothing illegal or worrisome was found in his system, although the medications he had been prescribed for pneumonia can have side effects. Prednisone, for example, can cause psychosis."

"Had Wade shown any signs of psychosis before the accident?"

"Not that I'm aware of."

"How much do you know about the accident itself?"

"Simply that it occurred and the nature of the resultant injuries: one person sustained a fatal blow to the head, two people were crushed, a fourth required a hand amputation at the wrist, and Mr. Havelock suffered psychologically. In prior interviews with plant managers and their representatives, I told them what I have told you.

"Please excuse me now. I must get back to work and don't wish to disturb her." Glancing toward Na again, Gina turned to leave.

"Yes, of course. Thank you very much, Gina." As she disappeared into the hall, Zeb's thoughts turned back to Wade. Having lost his own support system once, he understood what it meant to be unexpectedly alone and shared the nurse's concerns about depression.

Zeb had met Brice the first day of the PhD program. Her wild hair and thirst for the world were irresistible, and their lives quickly intertwined. Together they excelled in their coursework and tackled special projects of breadth and complexity. Among the graduate students, they were revered and respected.

Willingly and passionately, Zeb had assisted Brice with her

doctoral psychology research, sacrificing progress on his own. Gradually, her dissertation on modern business values mutated into a justification of those values. Scholarly criticisms transformed into affirmations, delighting executives she had connected with. One particular executive offered her a lucrative consulting position, which Zeb guessed included providing services and receiving benefits that invoked pangs of humiliation in him. Astoundingly, she accepted the executive's offer and vanished from Zeb's life, just like that.

Brice had asked for his support, he had given it, and then she rescinded the deepest love he had known. As a result, his interests and emotions aligned. Depressed and deflated, he lost all curiosity about the living and specialized in a topic that few academics considered worthwhile. Thereafter, his professional life became increasingly isolated and self-reliant.

Wade truly loved his job at the plant. Zeb was convinced of that. Disturbed by the accident at first, Wade was currently struggling with being mistrusted and stuck at home. Zeb concluded he could do more for a sullen Wade than a sleeping, impassive Rojana—who, by the way, had gotten herself into trouble by doing precisely what he had warned against. Zeb decisively gathered his papers and slipped out of the clinic.

As soon as he got in his car, he checked the radio for classical music. Only finding country, he turned the radio off and rolled the windows down. The cadence of the wind soothed his slight twinges of guilt. By the time he arrived at Wade's, Zeb was pure positivity. Lights from the kitchen indicated Wade was awake. Zeb quickly parked, hopped up to the door, and gave a purposeful knock.

"Hello! Good to see you again, Dr. Elmir!" Wade wore loose plaid pajamas and a fuzzy robe but didn't sound sleepy. Zeb guessed they were his all-day clothes. "Come on in. I'm simmering some curry. It won't be done for another hour, though. Try not to slobber, ha ha!"

"You're in good spirits," Zeb remarked as he removed his shoes. "Feeling better today?"

"I put everything in perspective. Pneumonia almost killed me a couple months ago, and demons could have killed me at the plant. Sure, I'm not at my best. I'm as dizzy today as I was yesterday. But hey, I'm alive, and I've got your help, too."

"True enough." Zeb meant it literally; Wade was close enough to being correct to merit a pass. Ghosts were often confused with demons. Not wanting to dampen Wade's cheer, Zeb skipped explaining the distinction. "You took your meds today?"

"Yes, Doctor, exactly as prescribed, Doctor."

"I'd like to see what you're taking, if that's alright."

"Sure thing. All my pills are in the bathroom cabinet. I really do take them exactly as prescribed," he said with a smirk. "Are you looking for anything particular?"

"No, no, I just didn't think to mark them down yesterday. What kind of curry?"

17

BOONE HAD EVERYTHING arranged for the researcher's potential visit by 11 AM. He liked to be prepared. Following Taryn's suggestion, he had pulled all the newspaper issues with accidents or injuries—a couple dozen—and stacked them in reverse chronological order. In addition, he reorganized the books and magazines on display and queued up an accurate but campy historical video a high school class had made a few years ago. Student videos aside, Boone took great pride in the museum and showed it off readily, even though it was one of those dinky, small-town, everyone-has-one places.

The museum's most popular artifact was its largest, and its sole concession to sensationalism. Just through the door, in front of the first support column, stood a stuffed black bear unrealistically posed in a face-off against two snarling raccoons. Boone didn't know the creatures' origins. Had they been shot while actually snarling at each other, or were they found dead by the side of the road? Regardless, the exhibit ate up too much space and was false advertising. It lured passing tourists by implying more exciting stuff lay hidden inside.

In truth, it was the museum's only animal exhibit, and from an eager, creature-loving kid's perspective, the rest of the museum was a letdown. Still, Boone couldn't bring himself to dump it. He had inherited it from the previous curator twenty years ago. It couldn't be moved safely and was virtually impossible to replace, so Boone hung on to it, tolerating the occasional "Laaaame" droned by disappointed children.

Items of greater historical value filled the rest of the museum's limited space. Wooden filing cabinets held copies of the town's intermittently published newspaper, the *Milton Courant*. Next to the cabinets, under a sign reading, ON THIS DAY IN . . ., a lighted glass case displayed issues from previous years. Boone rotated them out each morning, along with relevant artifacts like woodworking tools and trapping gear. If someone wanted to, they could visit the museum every day for a year and always see something different.

Photographs lined the walls, moving from daguerreotypes to tintypes on one side and from black-and-white to recent color photos on the other. Most of the older pictures were of the town itself and showed how quickly it had developed during the lumber boom. From one image to the next, paths became sidewalks and hitching rails became parallel parking. The more recent pictures were large prints of group photos taken during the annual Milton Town Picnic. A few of them had clear shots of Taryn's mother beaming brightly as she clung to her husband on sunny, happy days. Boone touched the frames, tweaking their already level-perfect alignment.

Feeling suddenly heavy, he sat down at his corner desk and rubbed his thighs. "My get up and go got up and went," he breathed. "Taryn's right: I should eat more protein for breakfast." At least he could relax the rest of the day. The only thing he had left to do was call his daughter during lunch and catch up on the day's political intrigues.

18

IT WAS DARK when Na awoke. Someone had strapped her into an inclined bed. She could only wiggle her feet, hands, and head. The rest of her, from her shoulders down to her ankles, was tightly bound by several wide straps that reminded her of seat belts. Hanging in the air over her legs was a silver plate suspended from the ceiling by a silver chain that split and attached to the plate in three places. A faint light shone off its sharp edge. Slowly and silently, the odd platter began to swing toward Na. Each swing peaked slightly nearer to her. It soon swung near enough to see it held a thin layer of coarse, white sand.

Why would someone do this?

The platter continued swinging back and forth on a trajectory set to slice the bridge of Na's nose. As it drew ever closer, she saw something else. A camouflaged spider squatted in the platter's center. Its translucent white body blended perfectly with the sand. Only its brown eyes stood out, making it unnoticeable until it was merely a foot away. *Maybe it's fake. Or dead. Please don't jump on my face.*

Completely restrained as she was, blowing seemed to be her only option. If she did it correctly and blew against the plate's bottom, she could keep the plate from hitting her. But if she missed the timing and blew across the top, she might propel the eerie spider onto her immobilized body. She decided to blow gently at first, hopefully with just enough force to counter whatever caused the swinging.

As the silver saucer approached, she blew a steady, soft stream of air, testing the sand and the spider. The sand didn't move, and the spider didn't stir, but neither did the swinging slow down. Away the plate swung and then back again. Na drew a deeper breath and blew harder. This time, the plate slowed just a little, and the spider wiggled a leg. *It's getting too close. Try again. Blow faster; just hit the bottom. This can work.*

Again the platter swung away, and again it approached. Na inhaled deeply, ready to blow, and saw the platter was empty. The spider was gone. She immediately lost her breath. *When did it fall? Where is it?* Had it leapt off at the far end and safely floated to the floor on a thin strand of webbing, or was it crawling along her pajamas, searching for unprotected skin? Panicked, she struggled, tossed, and shook against the straps. They were anchored securely and didn't give. She tried to scream for help and woke up instead.

Groggy from feeling like she had woken up twice, Na focused on what she knew was real to force the nightmare arachnid from her mind.

"What time is it?" she asked aloud. No one answered. She yawned and tried to stretch. She couldn't; she really was pinned to a bed. A single strap restrained her chest, and another fixed her right arm in place. A sickening recollection of the previous night surged into her mind. Something bad had happened, and now she was . . . where? Lifting her head, she made sense of her surroundings. It looked like a hospital room. She scanned her bandaged arm. *At least it's my dominant one,* she thought sarcastically. *Fuck that cursed cabin. No wonder the dentist stayed away. So much for my grand plan.*

She effortfully called out: "Hello? Hello!" Scuffing shoe soles on tile, much like dry skin rubbing paper, told her someone had heard. She dropped her head back onto the pillow.

A middle-aged man gleefully sprang into the room. "Welcome! How are you doing?"

"I don't know yet," she replied flatly. Na wasn't ready for a suspiciously upbeat people person who may or may not have a spider in his pocket.

"You're just waking up, aren't you? Let me say first that you're going to recover. I'm Dr. Charleston. Welcome to the Milton Medical

Wellness Clinic. You've experienced some arm trauma, a puncture wound, which led to symptoms of shock. That's why you passed out."

"I think I remember that."

"Good."

"How did I get here?"

"You'll have to ask my wife about that. I wasn't here when you were brought in. She's the head nurse. Her name's Gina."

"I don't remember her."

"You were unconscious. We're going to watch you tonight to ensure you are fully over the shock. I'll probably release you tomorrow."

"And my arm?"

"It's not broken. You will have a noticeable scar and perhaps nerve damage. We'll have to see how things go. If you do have nerve damage, you wouldn't feel it yet because you're on a strong analgesic. But either way, you will recover. You can move your wrist and fingers, right?"

"Uh, yeah."

"There, see? You don't have paralysis. That was the biggest worry. You've dodged the worst. As you recover, you'll want to inform us of any new symptoms, like burning, muscle spasms, a lack of sensation, and so on. But you're young. You'll heal."

"Uh, thanks. When can I—?"

"Let me get Gina. She can answer your other questions."

The doctor zipped out before Na could finish. She sighed and turned away from the door. Noticing an empty chair in the corner, she imagined what Dr. Elmir was doing, unsurprised that he wasn't there. *Maybe he's at the dentist's place. Maybe he's hanging out with Wade. Maybe he's browsing the internet. Maybe he's taking a nap, figuring that if I get a day off, he should too.* Her thoughts became less and less complimentary.

"Yes?"

"What?" Na exclaimed. The nurse had glided up to the bedside without Na noticing.

"I'm Gina. Dr. Charleston said you had questions?"

"Yeah, I do." Na paused to swallow and catch her breath. "Thank you. What happens next? Will I need a cast? A sling?"

"You'll be advised to wear a sling for comfort. It will help stop you from using the damaged muscles and thereby help you heal and control pain. Naturally, you'll be given painkiller and antibiotic prescriptions when you are discharged. You will also need to change the wound's dressing once or twice a day."

"Echhh. Can I get up, or at least sit up?"

"Now that you're awake, yes. I can get those for you." Nurse Gina swiftly unfastened both straps, ambidextrously undoing one with each hand.

"Thanks."

"Try not to move too much. And once you're back to sleep, we may refasten the straps to keep you from aggravating the injury."

"Okay. Um, the doctor said you were here last night. Do you know who brought me?"

"The person who dropped you off said he was not related to you, that he had found you next to the road and brought you here." Observantly, Nurse Gina added, "He may have purchased the flowers. Is there a card?"

"Flowers? Where?"

"On the table behind you. You should lie still. Allow me to check, please. No, there is no card."

"It wasn't Dr. Elmir?"

"I do not believe so. He came later this morning, after we were able to reach your hotel. Do you need anything else?"

"Oh. Uh, no. Thanks."

Na had a lot to digest. *No paralysis, scarred for life, out of shock, tied to a bed for safety, and not sure how I got here. Great. Ugh. I haven't called Mom. I should let her know everything's fine . . . sort of . . .*

Her phone had been thoughtfully placed on a nearby tray, next to the TV remote and call button. Na had no desire to relive her failure by watching the video she had taken and only checked her phone's call history. It was empty; no incoming or outgoing calls were listed. *I didn't dial 911? Crap. Who picked me up from the road?* Many potential answers were unnerving. She pushed them from her mind. *Better call Mom.* As she listened to the line ring, Na's determination returned. *I'll just touch base. I won't tell her where I am. If I tell her, she'll want to come get me, and I'm not leaving like this.*

19

NA COULDN'T TELL how hard she had knocked on Dr. Elmir's door. Thanks to the analgesic, she couldn't feel her knuckles. *Analgesic.* She snickered. *Is this normal? Is this how I think?* She tested herself: *I am Na. Na is me. Hello, Na.* She felt normal enough internally, but the brass "215" on the door had a dim, unreal quality. She remembered waking up that morning after a long, drug-induced sleep. She remembered tossing the mystery flowers she couldn't easily carry in the same hand as her backpack. She somewhat remembered being driven to the hotel by a hospital guy. *How long ago did I knock?*

"Na, come in. Sit here." Dr. Elmir dragged a chair to her and propped the door open. "That'll give you some air." He spoke sympathetically. "How are you doing? How is your arm?"

"I'm fine." She looked down at the navy-blue sling. It warmly and comfortably wrapped around her neck and shoulder, covering the gauze on her arm. "I'm still on drugs. They said I'll start to feel stuff soon." She sat down lightly. "How are you?"

"I'm glad you're okay. Are you hungry?"

"Tired. I need a nap." Saying "nap" triggered a yawn. She closed her eyes, turned her face to the side, and relished the sense of oxygen rushing from her lungs to her toes.

"Sounds like a good idea. We've had a busy couple days." Dr. Elmir plunked onto the bed across the room from Na.

"Yeah."

"So, can you talk about what happened?" he asked softly.

She replied sleepily. "I went to the cabin and found the blood. It

was really dark. I tripped when I was looking around, fell, and . . ."
She pointed her shoulder toward him. As she spoke, she realized her
blood now spattered the cabin too. Maybe a chunk of her flesh was
there as well, jammed inside the hollow metal bar that had punched
a hole through her like a cookie cutter. She was too woozy to be
bothered by the notion.

"I visited you at the clinic yesterday. You were knocked out, and
I didn't want to disturb you. Right now, I'm waiting for the mayor to
call me back. I'm hoping to tour the plant on Monday and see what
there is to see. Anyway, I have some news for you."

"News." Na repeated the word reflexively. Her transient mind
had wandered to the crispy bed sheets directly above her.

"The ghost that Sompob saw was wearing a cross of Toulouse."

"Across?" Her foggy attention hobbled back to the conversation.

"Here, see?" He opened a file on his laptop and walked it over
to show her a picture. "He was probably from Southern France and
may have been alive in the 1100s."

"He's a thousand years old?"

"He wouldn't feel a thousand years old. When people die, their
spirits leave our time. To them, time here can pass much more
quickly. I'll elaborate. One of the most common reports from near-
death experiences is a tunnel of light, with deceased relatives often
beckoning at the other end. Are those relatives trapped in the same
timeline as ours, waiting decades and decades for their loved ones
to die? I think not. To them, time is different because they're outside
our world. The flow of our time is linear, like a river. It constantly
flows in one direction. When a person dies, that person steps out
of the river, out of the flow of our time, into a different world. From
that spot on the riverbank, the deceased can look around and
immediately see others who have stepped out, whether they stepped
out upstream—in our past—or downstream—in our future. This
space outside the river has its own flow of time; just like next to an
actual river, one can walk upstream or downstream more quickly or

more slowly than the water flows.

"Ghosts are shadows cast by the dead as they pass near our river. We can sometimes see them, but we can't touch their shadows any more than we can touch our own. Separated from us in another world with another time, spirits are out of our reach, and we are out of theirs."

"If you say so." *Maybe that'll make sense after a nap.* Na lacked the energy to try to understand. "Why's he in Thailand?"

"I don't know, but it's a myth that ghosts only appear in places they are strongly connected to. They frequently do, but frequently doesn't mean only."

"Oh." Na's focus began slipping away again. *I wish I could control my dreams. Southern France would be nice.*

"Anyway, I can tell you're tired. Since you're here, though, let's go over a few things."

"Okay."

"You're hurt, so you're going to have to take it easy. You need a chance to recover. That said, I need your help. I can't do this study alone. If you feel up to it, there are things I'd like you to do."

"Sure." *Sitting on a beach, eating éclairs, and snoozing to the waves' rhythm . . .*

"You'll have to stick to a schedule and check in regularly so I know where you are and how you're doing. I'm going to be strict about that. You'll be on a short leash. Got it?"

"Yes."

"Good. We'll start tomorrow. There's a small-town picnic, an annual thing. It'll be a good chance to meet the locals and leaders. Well then, that's all. You'd better get some rest. Meet me downstairs in the office when you wake up. If I haven't seen you by dinner, I'll come get you to make sure you eat."

"Alright." Na got up to leave. *Do they have French toast here? Would they cook it for dinner?*

"By the way," added Dr. Elmir, "it's the hotel that was new."

"Hmm?"

"The New Mill Hotel."

"Haaaaaa."

Na shuffled out through the open door. She knew she should be upset about something but didn't care what it was. Her arm had begun to ache, and she wanted sleep. The gold lines in the carpet faded with her focus as she trod upstairs to 315's bed. Without taking off her shoes, she tenderly lay down on her back and closed her eyes. *This sling is so cozy* was her last waking thought.

20

NERVES ARE STUPID. *All they do is get in the way. They don't help you think. They don't make you stronger. They just sap your willpower until you crumple and fail. Damn them.*

Doug had chickened out. Bravely, perhaps, he had sprung into action when he found her bleeding on the pavement. Genuinely concerned, he only thought of her safety as he wrapped her arm, lifted her into his car, and drove her to the clinic. He hadn't even noticed what her hair smelled like. *Her hair.* And then, as he stood in the clinic's gift shop with a pen in his hand, he had chickened out on the card.

He overthought it and paralyzed himself: *Is it creepy that I found her? Will she think I was following her? Will she blame me because I told her that story? It was kind of my fault. Should I say, "I'm sorry, I hope you're okay"? I can't tell her how beautiful she is.* Surrendering to his nerves in the end, he handed the cardless flowers to a receptionist and fled.

At least he had her picture. He had stealthily and shamefully taken it the day they met, as she passed his storefront window on the way back to her hotel. Doug closed his eyes, squeezed his phone in his palm, and willed her to be well. *I hope you're not in pain. I hope they're treating you well. Please heal quickly.* He didn't really know her, but she deserved the best care. Everyone did.

He knew he was thinking about her too much; after all, they had only talked once. But he wasn't captivated by every young woman who entered his store. He dismissed flirtatious high school girls without a second thought, including seniors in his age range. But she stood out. There was something engaging about her beyond her beauty, and he couldn't help himself. He looked at her picture again.

Loser.

Is it too late to drop something off at the hotel? Doug wondered. *I could leave a box of Kokomyntz and a note. A handwritten note might make up for the flowers.* The hotel was right next to his store. Maybe he could find out her name, too. *First, I've got to write the note. What sounds caring in an authentic, winningly dashing way?*

21

THE SEDATED SUBJECT sat tied to a chair. He looked like a partly unwrapped strawberry ice cream bar after a bite had splintered its white chocolate shell. He was ready for scientific consumption. Positioned near the subject's chair was a surgical remnant of his amputated leg, a mangled chunk of muscle, bloody marrow, and a swatch of hairy skin. For scientific control, there was also a collection of random tissue from other people.

A person dressed in a surgical apron, gloves, and mask began narrating.

"The EEG indicates the subject's electrophysiological properties are acceptable. Before- and after-treatment comparison scans and findings from previous subjects have narrowed but not eliminated epiphenomenal brain activity. Activity known to be irrelevant has been marked on chart 0722C. Injections are to be given in the regions marked on chart 0722D. The subject is ready. Here we go, Descartes, into the realm of thought. Beginning the procedure. It is 4 PM."

The orbitofrontal and ventromedial prefrontal cortices were tricky to access. They were the brain's lower frontal areas, right behind the face. Because they differed greatly from human to human, the investigator believed they held great promise and were worth the effort to examine. Modern medicine's current technique for accessing them—endoscopic surgery through the nasal cavity—was much less destructive than the older, inelegant approach used by the investigator: sawing apart the subject's head. Sawing was simpler and more direct but had its own challenges. Only so much skull bone could be removed before a subject's eye sockets got in the way.

Thankfully, this subject's appearance after the experiment didn't matter. That had sped up the preparation a little and would make cleanup substantially faster. Post-op, the investigator planned to lift the subject's scalp, drop the excised skull shards inside, and tightly stitch the skin closed. In other words, to do the minimum necessary to prevent the subject from literally pouring his brains out. After chemically disrupting the indicated neural pathways, implanting four electrodes, and watching for effects on the subject and/or surrounding tissue samples, the whole lot would be medical waste.

The investigator found running such experiments to be the ultimate test of self-discipline. Brains floated in fluid they produced to protect themselves from bruising and decrease their weight. Thus, just like semicongealed gravy in plastic wrap, brains begged to be squeezed. It would be so easy to do; during these tests, the subjects' brains sat naked, exposed and alluring. Although surgical gloves dampened the tactile sensations somewhat, the investigator imagined squeezing one to be intensely satisfying, far beyond that of crushing a warm, overripe tomato until its seeds squirted between the fingers. Hence, the investigator needed self-discipline. The tiniest gratuitous pinch could set off an unthinkable chain of events, ranging from wasting a subject's precious data to the forced cessation of further experimentation.

"Starting inhibitory injections, moving upward from the underside. Topside-down injections have previously yielded unsatisfactory results." That had been a bad day. The subject had begun thrashing, then grabbed the investigator and shook, unwittingly stirring the syringe around like a piña colada straw. To hide that damage, the investigator had to stage a convincing accidental car jack collapse. Setting that up wasted hours from his finite pool of time.

Only small, thirty-gauge needles had been prepped; it was fine work, and with preliminary maps plotted, tiny needles were needed to pinpoint the injection locations. The targets were brain fingerprints—specific ganglia that were different in everyone. Small needles also lessened bleeding and collateral damage, making it easier to sift through the data and determine which responses came from the chemical's neurological effects and which came from the injection process itself. A single errant stab could drastically change the outcomes.

The investigator pivoted the syringe on the rim of the subject's brainpan, a practiced technique that kept the needle steady while permitting it to move freely from point to point. He leaned in close, inches away from the mass of tangled cells that comprised the subject's essence. Because live brains were odorless, the only scent in the air came from the investigator's own breath, sweetened by lunch's soy-glazed veal chops. He could see the subject's blood vessels pulsate after each heartbeat—or maybe that was an illusion, a visual effect arising from intense concentration. The mind often saw what it wanted to see, the investigator knew. From across the room, party trays at social functions might seem full of chocolate chip cookies. In fact, they almost always contained stale wheat crackers.

"The injections are completed. No events. Now positioning the probes and starting electrical stimulation. Let's see if today's our lucky day."

The investigator gently set two probes on each cortex. Rudimentary yet invaluable for neural research, the probes were no more than pieces of metal with wires leading back to a control box on a wheeled cart. Giving the cortices controlled shocks would activate the pathways modified by the injections, fundamentally forcing the subject's train of thought to jump its tracks and follow new rails. Using a bloody, latex-covered knuckle that left a smear, the investigator flipped the probes' switches. Instantly, the subject's body shuddered as if his skin had exhaled. It almost looked like extreme nervousness. In contrast, the many instruments monitoring the leg remnant and assorted flesh remained silent.

"Nothing. Disappointing and unsurprising. Confirmed:

the neural network must be hard-lined to receive commands. Displacement has no consequences. One moment." The investigator held out a hand. It cast a single shadow. The investigator peered at the subject's healthy leg. It cast two shadows. The investigator moved urgently. "Halting the procedure. Turning off the probes and monitors. Shutting down."

Having depowered the equipment, the investigator peered again at the subject's leg and double-checked the other tissues. With a relieved tone, the investigator reported, "One shadow. All clear. Beginning cleanup and disposal. Additional subjects are being primed. Sidenote: Maintain vigilance. Alertness equals safety."

22

NA DRIFTED, CONSCIOUS yet disconnected, underneath a warm blanket of painkillers on her hotel mattress. She felt at one with and apart from herself. In the way of deep sleep, she knew without thinking: *Nothing is important. Just sleep. Soak in it. Absorb it. Be everything.* Her dozing mind had closed off Milton and extended beyond itself, dreamily touching faraway corners that felt real. *Parties. Swamps. Dressers. Glaciers.* Indistinct, half-dreamt objects and locations meandered in and out of her peripheral vision.

Then an entirely new sensation, a prickling fizzle in her right triceps, yanked off the blanket and slung her back to the New Mill Hotel. It didn't exactly hurt, but it felt wrong and disquieted her. The fizzle stuttered more on than off, like a laggy internet video. She rolled onto her left side to raise the wound and help her blood flow. Na had never been injured like this before. Her worst injuries had been bruises, twists, and sprains from softball. She had no idea of what to expect.

She tried not to worry. *The doctor warned me the meds would wear off. It's probably that. It doesn't burn or itch, and it's not twitching. It's probably normal.* Still sleepy, Na checked the clock. Dinner was more than an hour away. *Okay, it's just hunger. My arm wants food to heal, the same as a spasming muscle wants nuts or a banana. Take it easy, arm; relax and wait. Food is coming soon.*

As she fell back asleep, the prickling fizzle gradually lessened and faded away.

PART 3
RECEPTION

23

SATURDAY

LIVELY VOLUNTEERS OFFERED tub after tub of mayonnaise-based cuisine, challenging Na to sample pasta mixtures, cubes of baked potatoes, salads, and gluten-free bean jumbles. Na felt stronger today, but not strong enough for that.

Haphazardly arranged tables occupied the center of the flat, grassy park. Few had benches or chairs. Most tables were serving stations, leaving people to eat standing up or on blankets spread around the perimeter. Hand-drawn signs and occasional donation boxes on the tables read, GIRL SCOUTS, ROTARY, MILTON PRESBYTERIAN, and so on. Na's sling gave her an easy out when rejecting their heaping scoops; with only one free hand, she obviously couldn't hold a paper plate and eat.

The sling aided her in other ways, too. She had brought only one shirt that could be easily donned in her state: an immodest spaghetti-strap top intended for sleeping on hot nights. With the sling draped over it, she did not feel too exposed for what was technically a workday.

Dr. Elmir had said that the Milton Town Picnic, conveniently located just down the street, would be a brilliant opportunity to ingratiate themselves with the town's leadership. Na couldn't disagree. Although Dr. Elmir had talked to most on the phone already, Na had yet to meet or speak with any of them. Her attendance, like Dr. Elmir's, was not for pleasure. Nevertheless, Na could tell from Dr. Elmir's affable nods and chitchat that he was attempting to innocuously blend in. His efforts were wasted. Dr. Elmir had a stereotypically academic air that marked him as an outsider, not unlike a professional basketball player in street clothes.

"Are you sure you don't want me to hold a plate so you can try something?" Dr. Elmir asked.

"I'm okay," Na answered without looking at him. "My appetite's a little off, is all."

"You're probably right not to push it, then. Let me know if you change your mind. Some of this stuff is pretty good. It's better than, uh, what we've had." He glanced around slyly, presumably for eavesdroppers. "Ah, and that's them up ahead, at the table with a banner."

"The MAYOR'S TABLE banner? I see it," Na replied dryly.

Circling around a small group of conversing picnickers, Na sighted Doug inside a small tent at the edge of the festivity. He had a functional, old-time taffy puller with which he had spellbound a cluster of children. The simple movements of the puller's counterrotating arms caught and stretched shimmering sugar rope back onto itself, almost like an optical illusion. Na became as entranced as the children, momentarily. The sling tugging the back of her neck snapped her out of it and reminded her that she did not want to visit Doug today. She didn't blame him for what had happened. Rather, she hadn't concocted an unembarrassing explanation for it.

Powering onward, Na led the way. Dr. Elmir, who kept stopping to sample dishes, lagged slightly behind. As she approached the mayor's table, she heard a stout man seated at the table's near end proclaim, "That's why we do this, to ease the pressures of keeping pace with a changing marketplace." Except for a healthy-looking woman with wavy, shoulder-length blond hair, the speaker's companions gazed elsewhere. "Doctor Elmir!" the man thunderously announced as he rose, making Na and everyone else at the table jump.

"Mayor Handsom?" Dr. Elmir responded from somewhere behind Na.

"Right you are! Herbie Handsom, at your service. Everyone's here! Come meet them," he welcomed with a wide arm sweep. Indicating each person with an open palm, he went around the table. "My efficient assistant, Taryn Hales, whom you've spoken to." The blond woman nearly bowed.

"Her father, our museum's curator and an elder statesman of sorts, Boone Hales." In the same manner as his daughter, a thin, casually dressed man nodded deeply.

"Tim Rawls, our esteemed chief of police, who has held his position longer than any predecessor, and finally, Sarah Rawls, his wife and dignified council member."

The last two, in outfits matching their titles, smiled and waved quickly to both Dr. Elmir and Na. Na smiled back and added a mental hash mark to her tally of married couples who could pass as siblings.

"Greetings, everyone. I'm Zebediah Elmir. This is my research intern, Rojana Bensen. We're doing a study on possible intersections between culture and industrial acciden—"

The mayor hastily interrupted. "Horrible things, yes, and not really proper picnic conversation, if I may say. Some even wanted to cancel the picnic and hold a memorial instead." He side-eyed someone at the table; Na couldn't tell who. "Here in Fulton County, and especially Milton, we need every tourist dollar and blue-collar job we can get. No, it's better we cheerfully continue marching after we've safely and speedily learned who was responsible. That's why you have my enthusiastic support, Dr. Elmir." Raising his fork for emphasis, he concluded, "Things will be back to normal soon!"

Boone deftly refocused the discussion. "Speaking of, I was told to expect you at the museum. Is that correct, Dr. Elmir?"

"Absolutely, on Taryn's suggestion. She's been invaluable. We plan to visit as soon as we can."

Boone winked at Taryn and noted, "Normally, that would mean Monday. We're closed on Sundays. It might be better, though, if you weren't disturbed by the public, right? I could open for you tomorrow, let you look over our records at your leisure."

"Works for us," Dr. Elmir replied. Spontaneously, he cocked his head at someone Na couldn't see. "Excuse me, everyone. We meant to chat a while, but there's a person I recognize. We'll be in touch."

"Yes, please, yes," said the mayor, reasserting himself. "Go ahead. You know how to reach us if you need our help!"

Na was already trotting to catch up to Dr. Elmir by the time Mayor Handsom finished speaking. She found herself moving more slowly across the soft lawn than Dr. Elmir, even though she wore springy cross-trainers and he wore leather boat shoes. The painful prickling in her arm had returned. She assumed the fizzling was part of the healing process, but it made her wonder how people learned to ignore chronic pain. *Is pain always there, in the back of a person's mind? Does it get filtered out automatically, like the smells and noises in our own homes?* She jogged to catch up.

They headed to the far side of the park, opposite the street side from which Dr. Elmir and Na had entered. The main parking lot was there, and among its many vehicles stood a large man leaning against a silver pickup truck and waving. "Dr. Elmir!" Na heard him call in a boisterous, uneven voice.

Dr. Elmir's been making the rounds. Everyone knows his name, she mused.

Reaching the large man, Zeb responded in a friendly tone, "How are you doing, Wade? Better?"

"Maybe, ha ha. That's how it goes, right? I felt stable this morning. Now that I'm here, I'm not sure. I'm waiting to see if I can sample what everyone's brought or if I should just drive back home. Who's this?"

"Oh, you two haven't met. Wade, this is my research assistant, Rojana Bensen. Na, this is Wade."

"Good to mee—" Na gagged and almost spit up. She gulped, breathed a couple times, and tried again. "Good to meet you. Sorry. Dr. Elmir, my arm. May I?"

"Please, yes. Do you need a hand?"

"No. Thanks." Na shambled to the edge of the lot and sat on the curb where the lawn and pavement met. Maybe she could have overheard what Dr. Elmir and Wade said from there. She didn't try. Her stomach stopped churning upon sitting, but her arm kept buzzing. She leaned backward onto her left arm and deliberately turned her attention toward the picnic. A swarm of people moved around like bees circling a syrupy flower. It reminded Na of her bustling college campus. There was always someone doing something odd in the quad.

"What am I doing here?" she asked the distant flock of chattering strangers.

24

BOONE, AS HE liked to be called, watched Na scan the news articles he had carefully assembled days earlier. He hadn't expressed the slightest annoyance at meeting her on his day off.

"Loggers have the highest fatality rate, higher even than construction workers and roofers," he pointed out. "Milton's had its share of loss. Nothing like New York's Triangle Fire or the fertilizer explosion in Texas, though."

Na appreciated his educated interjections. Boone had been incredibly helpful. With his aid, she had a chance to be back at the hotel before lunch. "What about 'Bear mauls children'? Are animals extra aggressive around here?"

"No more than anywhere people build homes in the forest."

"Hmm." Na skimmed another issue. "This would be easier if the articles were searchable."

"Somewhere, someone in City Hall has a stickie with AUTHORIZE DIGITIZING *MILTON COURANT* scribbled on it. It's probably buried under more urgent stickies, like CLEAN LUNCHROOM MICROWAVE," Boone remarked sardonically.

"None are *obviously* relevant, but all of them *might* be." Na unzipped her backpack and removed her phone, which had been woefully underused lately. "I'll take pictures of them all. Better safe than sorry."

"Can I do that for you? Two arms are better than one," Boone offered.

"Yeah, okay. Thanks." Na passed her phone, and they switched places. She sat in Boone's chair, and Boone stood in front of the glass display case. "Please try to get as close as you can to each article without taking more than one picture per story."

"Yep, will do."

"Come to think of it," Na transitioned, "you might know what I'm after off the top of your head. Do you mind?"

"Shoot."

Na set her notebook on the desk and took out a pen. Handwritten notes would suffice for an unofficial, unsanctioned interview, even if the process made her arm twinge. "What's the vibe here? Is the town dying out, or is it a strong community with its own identity?"

"It's seen changes. There are fewer logging and hunting jobs, more tourism and small-farm jobs. There are pictures on the wall over there that show the progression. But Milton still feels like Milton. In many ways, it's the same as when I was a kid."

"Does life seem easy or hard here? Simple and serene or a battle to survive?"

"Sometimes one, sometimes the other. We've never been wiped out by a storm, but there have been tough stretches when it felt like we had to fight."

Intrigued, Na pressed on. "Like what? Budget crises? Lyme disease?"

"More like strings of terrible events. Bad things come in threes: a scandal at City Hall, an E. coli outbreak at the elementary school, a group of elderly friends dying off together. Chains like that can touch everyone in multiple ways. It leaves you wondering"—Boone set Na's phone down—"if there's more death than life. But maybe that's me getting old and time doing what it does."

Na understood. "I'm sorry."

"No, I'm sorry. My wife, Taryn's mother . . . Let's just say things don't work out like you hope. Here in Milton, it's easy to hold on when things are going well. There isn't a lot of development. Nooks where people's hearts connected stay the same for years. Nooks so profoundly important to you that you wonder if they feel special to strangers too."

"Sometimes they do," she consoled.

"Yeah." Boone resumed taking pictures. "Having reminders everywhere can lessen your losses and keep you moving forward. It tells you who you were and how your gifts came to be. It's different from city people managing loss by chasing fads. Chasing the new is diversion without reflection; it's treating everything as equally important. That's not my style. Here."

Boone unhooked three photos from the wall and carried them to Na.

"Each year at the picnic, more and more people want to be in the town photo. When my wife was in it, you could tell it was her. That's her, there. Now it's getting crowded. It's hard to see who's who, even on bigger prints. That's not because the population is booming. It's not. Whatever it is, nostalgia or fresh air and farm life, there's an increase in Milton cheer. Everybody's participating. You were at the picnic. What did you think?"

"The mayor is a chase-the-new person."

Boone guffawed. "Yes, he is."

"I didn't notice much more than that. But from these newspapers and what you're saying, maybe Milton doesn't have what we're looking for after all."

"What is it you're after?"

Na gave an answer Dr. Elmir couldn't whine about. "A pattern of tragedy, to see how one can lead to others."

"Yeah." He nodded. "That doesn't sound like here. But I'm not omniscient. I don't know as much as my daughter might have said."

"I'm sure you do."

"Finished. That's it for your photos, Na."

"Thank you very much." She stashed her phone and notebook back in her bag. "I should get going. If you remember something, you can reach Dr. Elmir or me at the New Mill Hotel."

"I'll just call. It's a tall hotel; you'd be hard to reach."

"Haa haa." *Grandpa jokes.* "Have a good day, Boone."

Since her arrival in Milton, warm weather with a cooling breeze had encouraged strolling about. Today was equally hospitable. Not knowing how long her endurance would last as the day wore on, Na had packed light for the walk to and from the museum. But she was still able to move briskly and was motivated by hunger, so she marched purposefully along the street and contemplated what she'd learned.

Milton might not have what they were looking for. *But if it doesn't, does anywhere?* She wondered if ghosts came and left the way Mae Nak roamed Bangkok—if they could travel the world or if they were stuck hanging around particular spots, like the lumberjack supposedly did. Perhaps there were two types of spirits, travelers and settlers. *If yes, which attacked Sompob?* Telling them apart could help Sompob decide what to do with his house. Maybe it was safe for him to go back. It was a nice house.

But right now, they were helping Wade. If Wade had seen traveling ghosts, there was no way to find them. If, however, they were after stationary ghosts, someone else should have seen them too. Perhaps there were numerous stories about a single set of Milton ghosts that never ventured far from their homes or graves. The ones Wade saw might even be related to the lumberjack. *Or maybe there are more ghosts than we think. Maybe there's more danger than we think.* Na shivered.

She went back to the basic questions she had. *Are ghosts dead people or shadows of people that personify specific traits?* She was not sure which would be worse. If ghosts were dead people, that potentially made them thinking, planning, vengeful, self-righteous sadists with supernatural abilities and the power to follow through on their hate. If ghosts were nasty reflections of people's dark sides, they were evil but restricted. Reflections would probably attack indiscriminately without plans. They might chase, but they wouldn't consciously choose targets.

One question rose to the forefront of her thoughts: *Are all ghosts malicious?* She hadn't heard of explicitly benevolent ghosts. They might be rare, reported less often, or less likely to interact with living people. *Perhaps something draws certain kinds of people to becoming ghosts, like dark motivations or obsession bordering on insanity, like Mae Nak.*

"Hi. Uh, how's your arm?"

The sudden question startled Na. She furrowed her brow as she processed having been asked a question.

"Doug from Stuffs, remember?"

"Yeah, I know." She relaxed. "How are you?"

"How are you? How's your arm?"

Na shrugged. "It's healing."

"Good. I hope it's not bad. I'm sorry about that, your arm. I told you that story. I knew you might go there. It's not safe, and then you went—"

"You know how I hurt my arm?" Na stepped back.

"Well, yeah. I found you and drove you to the doctor. You might not remember. You were passed out." Doug looked down and scratched the back of his head.

"Weird, but you might have saved my life."

"I wasn't following you or anything," he offered. "The dentist's is near mine. I can see it from my window. That's partly how I know about it. I thought I saw a light, so I went and checked. Usually it's drunk high schoolers, but I knew it might be you. And you were by the road, totally out of it—"

"Thanks. For checking and for helping," Na added firmly.

"So. Look, I'm sorry. I should have warned you. I practically talked you into going."

"It's not your fault I tripped."

Doug winced. "It kinda is."

"Wait. Did you buy me flowers?" The question came out more accusatory than Na intended.

Doug winced again. "I'm sorry. I'm not great at this."

"Great at what?"

"I want to make it up to you. I want to show you something, something real, and this time I'll come with to make sure you know what's going on."

"Something real?" Na asked cynically.

"Historically real, at least. Maybe you won't like it, but it's true that I know lots of stories, tales other people don't know or wouldn't think of telling. This place has stories too."

A sparkle of hope kindled in Na. "Okay." She wasn't quite ready to discard Milton after all.

"Okay?"

"Yeah, okay. I should rest today. Can we do it tomorrow?"

"Sure. It'll be late, like after nine."

"That's okay."

"I'll pick you up from the hotel. Oh, and what's your name?"

"Na," she said over her shoulder as she walked away.

"Na-ah? I'll see you tomorrow, Naa."

25

SINCE THE PICNIC, when Dr. Elmir had introduced her to a table's worth of people he already knew, Na had felt out of the loop. The world had fast-forwarded ahead while she recovered in bed. In that time, Dr. Elmir had rapidly converted the hotel's business center into a duplicate of his university office. Mind maps and correspondence she knew nothing about were scattered everywhere. Without being in the know, she couldn't tell if Dr. Elmir's research was heading in the right direction.

She resorted to an apologetic tone when she asked Dr. Elmir for a detailed update as soon as he returned from touring the manufacturing plant where Wade worked. Dr. Elmir's solemn response was disconcerting, unsurprising, and reiterated how awful people could be.

"OSHA has accepted the factory management's version, which was buttressed by what the mayor said his own investigation concluded. They claimed there were no managerial lapses and no mechanical failures. A lone employee behaved unprofessionally and set off a chain of events leading to four casualties. Essentially, an overexcited Wade interfered with his coworkers' duties and misused the freshly refurbished equipment by pressing buttons he wasn't supposed to touch. Their angle against Wade isn't personal, however. His behavior is being ascribed to a health-related delirium caused by serious illness and preexisting conditions."

"Did you uncover anything that proved Wade's version?"

"No, and I didn't think I would. I went there to check four

things. One, I wanted to see the layout myself to better visualize what Wade described. Two, I looked for signs of electrical or mechanical malfunctions. There were no scorch marks, no loose bits of machinery, nothing. Three, I wanted to see how well the victims' blood had been cleaned. People don't like tidying up areas they think are cursed. An incomplete, rushed job may have meant the crew was scared. As it was, the sites were spotless, even where the unfortunate pair had been crushed. Finally, I wanted to observe whoever escorted me, which turned out to be a security guard. He was upset about his coworkers, but not distraught or jittery. He communicated clearly and congruently. If he's heard gossip about ghosts, it didn't bother him."

"You couldn't ask directly because you didn't want to start a rumor if there wasn't one already," Na remarked.

"Correct."

"They won't let Wade come back, will they?"

"No."

"What's next for us?"

"Well, I intend to approach the injured worker, the one who lost his hand. He deserves as much time to heal as I can spare. I'll wait a couple days longer before speaking to him. In the meantime, there are a few leads from your newspapers to look into, and I can't ethically leave Wade to his own devices yet. I at least owe him a couple informal counseling sessions, which might be all I can do. The rest will be watching to see how the story develops over time. I'll do that by monitoring social media and staying in touch with the contacts we've made."

"Are you saying we're almost done?"

"Perhaps. Right now the sole witness is Wade. As you know firsthand, most ghost sightings boil down to one person's word. If his coworker adheres to his statement in the report, then maybe we are."

Doug's invitation couldn't have come at a better time. They hadn't learned anything, and to top it off, she hadn't contributed. Her main role had been an ineffectual damsel in distress. She recalled the blood and dried biological fluids covering her arm. Everything about the wound disgusted her. *Boone was right about things not happening as planned*, she thought in frustration.

Na let Dr. Elmir get back to puttering in his makeshift office and set about preparing for a clandestine night excursion, which, according to the rules of random chance, *had* to pan out. *Unlucky streaks don't last forever. Things can only get better.*

26

CRYPTICALLY, DOUG HAD only told Na he wanted to show her "woods." Less than an hour's drive and hike later, they were positively deep in the woods. A canopy of branches and leaves obscured the moon and stars, leaving Na with absolutely no orientation. Without landmarks, she had no way of telling how much ground they had covered. She couldn't even guess where they were relative to the town. And she was following a man she hardly knew further and further from the road where they had parked. *Why do I keep doing dicey things? What happened to my rule about public places?*

"What's in your backpack?" Na asked nonchalantly.

"Survival gear. Rope, a knife, stuff like that. Nature can be dangerous. If you sprain an ankle or meet a wendigo, you need to be ready."

"Wendigo?"

"People-eater. A cannibalistic man-beast."

"You're not helping."

"We're getting close. People do illegal things where we're going. I'm taking us the back way so we don't surprise anyone. Coming up the main path, we could stumble across someone, or someone could stumble across us."

Na's heart skipped a beat. "Who else will be there?"

"No one, hopefully. It's not a hangout. It does get used, though, and I don't want a confrontation. It'll make sense when we get there."

"It's on private property?"

"Not as far as I know. It's treated like public land, anyway."

If they were following a trail, it was hidden from Na. Doug

continued trekking along the unmarked earth at an automaton's pace. She didn't have a lot of options. Through her actions if not her emotions, she had chosen to trust Doug. Na inhaled a lungful of soil-scented air and kept following, splitting time equally between watching her footing and assessing the shadows. Each gnarled branch knuckle her flashlight swept over wore a bleak grimace.

"It's really dark," she mustered after nearly tripping on the undergrowth.

"Yeah, it's perfect."

"Do we need to be quiet? Maybe I should have asked that before."

"Nah. We can be as loud as we want. By now, we'd know if anyone was there."

"How would we know?"

"We've nearly arrived." He looked over his shoulder. "You still alright?"

"I think so."

Although she heard disquiet in her own voice, Doug took her response at face value. "Cool."

For all she could tell, they were being hunted. Faint swishes from intermittent breezes confirmed that Na's ears functioned, but the impenetrable darkness remained. Motionless things didn't make noise. *Do predators really go after the sick and injured?*

For better or worse, this time she wasn't outdoors alone. Thin and a foot taller than she, Doug was unimposingly fit. He marched assertively. Watching his sure movements, Na reminded herself that she had no reason to distrust him. *Worry about actuals, not maybes.*

"This is it," Doug announced. "Stay close; there's a small drop here. And watch out for sharp objects."

They stood at the edge of a clearing about forty feet wide. It was round and sunken like a crater, with a lip that dipped down and a mound in the center. The mound had the odd silhouette of a pile of turtles, and the earth everywhere was black with patches of light gray. It smelled stale and old, leathery and dead.

"Can you tell what it is?" Doug quizzed.

Na stared into the heavens. The moon and stars were welcome sights, but they did not reveal where she was. "A bonfire for, like, high school parties?"

"Half right. It's a burn pit, an antique burn pit."

"Antique?"

"Hundreds of years old. It was part of the fur trade. After skinning and cleaning their kills, hunters burned the carcasses here. As hunting decreased, people burned other things too. Mattresses. Large pets. Assorted junk."

Na retched as painful fizzling flared from her wound again. To conceal her distress, she sat on the edge of the pit and kept talking normally. "Burning trash? That's the illegal thing people do here?"

"Yep. That can mean a hefty fine. Or massive embarrassment, depending on the mattress."

"Gross. Funny, but gross."

"Sure you're alright?"

"Just lightheaded. It's my arm," she said dismissively. "Anyway, tell me more."

"The pit's marked with death. You can smell it. If the forest has a guardian spirit, this is where it would be angriest."

"Mm-hm. So, you come here a lot? What kinds of stuff have you found?"

"All kinds over the years. What I wanted to show *you* is the bones. The ground is covered in ash, but dig down, and there's lots and lots of bones. Different sizes and colors from every kind of creature that's ever roamed these woods."

"Like?" Na wasn't all right. The electrical fizzling in her triceps crescendoed to an unintelligible chant, ensnaring her consciousness. Wanting to listen to Doug, she aimed her flashlight directly at him. He scuffed the dirt with his toe to simulate digging, gesticulating and describing skulls and fangs he had unearthed, but she couldn't absorb his words. Crackling hooks of pain yanked her concentration out of phase. Doug flattened into smudged mattes and faded into an intangible mirage. The cadence of his voice receded to a distant echo. Her flashlight, too, dimmed down to nothing.

She lifted her left hand to shake its batteries; her hand was empty. The night sky clouded up, softening, blurring, and then smothering its twinkling residents. Na found herself isolated and stranded.

The air stank of damp rot. Mist swirled and settled around her. Within the mist, vertical humanoid shadows formed. Two, three, four shadows. Na psychically yelled, *No more!* The shapes' hollow white eyes met hers, or maybe stared past her. She couldn't turn to check. She was ill and dizzy and didn't want to. These four shapes were enough. They were dead. They were very, very dead, incomplete mannequins of despair in modern tatters.

One shape, the furthest, turned and floated off. A second drifted forward and encroached. It was indistinguishable and real, nebulous and defined. A long, deep-brown coat hung over its incoherent feminine body. It reached out to touch her with a murky, dim gray finger. Its skin rippled and pulsated steadily, ready to pop and dissipate into nothing. Na closed her eyes and braced to scream with all her might.

A force pressured her ears and drew her eyes back open; the stars reappeared. Na was lying on her backpack. She sat up, retrieved her flashlight from the weeds at her flank, and squinted to clear her vision. Doug howled again.

"Naa! Get up, Na! NOW!" He was lying on his side about where she had seen him last. How long had she been absent? He pointed and cried, "Get up, move!"

Na needed time. "What? Why? You get up."

"I can't."

"What?"

"I can't. Just— Get up and *move*. Move!" He jabbed his index finger impatiently at the adjacent trees.

Na traced the line he drew and hoarsely whispered, "Krasue." A hovering, severed head glided toward her. A rainbow mass of soft glands and visceral organs dangled from its neck without bones to support them. Gravity should have ripped the heavy flesh off its flimsy esophageal tube. Instead, the wobbling guts swung along with the bouncing head, clapping together, flopping apart, and clapping together again. Such ghosts had different names in different places. In Na's family, they were called Krasue.

What was more, Na recognized the gory jellyfish. It bore the same face—but more distinct—as she had seen moments before on the encroaching shadow. She had no opportunity to deduce why its appearance had changed. Although suddenly armless, it kept coming for her. Its goal, according to Thai folklore: peeling open Na's belly and feeding.

Na desperately shook out her joints and staggered to Doug. His left leg was stalk straight, and he was pressing his hand into his hip. "What is it?"

"I don't know." His voice was distraught. "It just went numb and I fell. I can't move it."

She glanced at Krasue. It followed her and was gaining. "We need to go. Let me help." Na offered her good hand as leverage so Doug could pull himself up. On touching, his body trembled and gasped. She dragged his limp arm skyward until his right knee took over and brought him fully to his feet.

"W-T-F. It's better."

She squeezed Doug's sweaty, icy hand and didn't let go. "Can you run?"

"Not yet."

"Me neither."

Clasping each other for support, they unsteadily trotted across the rough, scrap-strewn pit. The gruesome head weaved and spun in place. Looking backward and nearly tripping, Doug asked, "Will it chase?"

"Don't know. Keep going."

"What the hell is it?"

"Krasue."

"A what?"

"Cursed spirit, doomed to hunger. It kills and eats people."

"Great. Wendigos don't exist, but that does." Doug led them down the main path, a neglected, partially overgrown driveway. "So, what, are you a ghost expert?"

"I watch a lot of movies," she sidestepped. "Don't slow down. Keep going." The further they ran, the better she felt. Her pain simmered down to a hum. "Where's your truck?"

"Ten minutes away? I think?" Coming to a paved road, they veered right and kept to the shoulder. "It wasn't supposed to be like this. What the actual fuck is going on?"

"Listen. Don't go back," Na commanded. "Daytime or nighttime, don't go back. There's something wrong about it."

"I wasn't ready." Doug's voice cracked.

Na hoped he wasn't fractured inside as well. *You never know how you'll react until you live it. We're more fragile than we like to think.* "You were right, Doug," Na said supportively. "There was lots of anger back there. That's why you can't go back. And thanks for waking me up. You saved me again."

"No," he rasped, "you saved me."

27

MY KNIFE IN their hips. Twisting grinds the blade edge, crunches collagen and ligament. *Pecadors.* Traitors, blasphemers, malefactors, sirens, all wail and leak and die. My knife's purpose. It finds the spot in one stick. Lodged in sinew. It moves when they wriggle in their chains. They want to shake it out. They try. It stays. It never slips, never slides until I pluck it out. When I pluck, it never catches, never chips. It draws out clean. All their blood, and the blade is clean. The handle is sticky. The blade is clean. My knife is lost.

It is not here. Someone keeps it. I hunt. People move. People mix. They take and carry and drop. One has it. One has my *cotèl.* I will find him and name him. My knife is not his. I am his judge.

I cannot lift it. I will find it. I will lift it. There is a way. Others touch. Others move. Others, like me and not. Corrupt. Crazed. Sinners all. I watch and they do what I cannot. There is a way. I will learn. All sinners will end. Not being, they will not sin. By my knife.

Others congregate. There is wrongness, pain *estranh*, where they collect. Corrupt and careless, they answer summoners. I go between alone. Safer. More control. Safe to test. Now is a time to test. There is a way. I go between, alone, far from others. I go between to . . .

Un ostal, in an empty room. Letters like mine, not mine, on walls. One pecador lives. Nearby, I sense him. Likenesses of more on walls. No crucifix. No faith. A gift, a chance. Providence. I will read him and test him. Divine hand led. I am thankful. From him may I learn. There is a way.

He sleeps, the pecador. Older than I and foolish. Uncovered in bed. Sweating and dreaming impiously. Patchy skin. Evil. I hear his heart's aberrant cackles. Feel them. He will feel my lesson. My knife instructs best. No knife. There are other ways. Until I lift, there are other ways. Others have shown.

No voice, no words. With fire of purpose, he will fear, understand, and die. By my hand, by His will. Wiser now, I will not fail Him here. In two parts he sleeps, unbelieving. *Pecador.* Time for him to know. Time to separate.

Bowels are slow. Bowels are agony. With my hand, I begin. His life inside him fights. My fist halts his flow. He clenches and curls. A baby. He hurts. He turns. He wakes. I greet him. He cannot endure. In misery he squirms, as those I chained. As those, he is held. Coward. His grime sears me. I withstand. I will win. I have no flesh. Only searing. My fire will outburn his. I do not fear. I will not lose again. Never.

He is desperate. He faces me. Pecador or innocent, desperation overtakes. His essence resists. Shoves back. Harder, my fist penetrates. A baby, he shrieks. Cloudy tears. He is sickening. Disgusting. He stinks. I force myself closer. My same arm, searing, my elbow to my hand inside his gut to his heart. His beats ripple into me. My fire splits him. Pushes apart. My face teaches him. This is his. He earned what I give. He cries more, cries out. Too late for faith. He separates. His first part leaves; his second part stays. The searing ends. He drops, dead like me and not. He is gone. I am not. I win.

I learn and exit from between. No knife, same end. Defiled by him, I cannot bathe. I feel his stain. Knife is pure. Knife is clean. First I will find it. Second I will lift it. Third I will use it. Until He calls, it will grind and crunch and drain them all. There is a way.

28

A VISITOR POUNDED unrelentingly. Zeb straightened his sleepwear and cracked open the door, hiding by standing beside the frame and leaning. "It's early, Na. *Really* early." Her grubby clothes suited her droopy, drained posture.

"I can't sleep. Tell me how they work. Those articles you had me read didn't say. You're wrong, but part of what you said is true. I mean, I think."

"I'm not ready to get up. Breakfast is hours away."

"I don't want to come in. Just tell me," she beseeched.

Utterly defeated by her insistence and resistance, Zeb surrendered his goal of maintaining Na's impartiality. *True impartiality is an ideal anyway, not an achievable goal*, he consoled himself. "Fine. Then we're both going to sleep. You look awful."

"Deal."

He left the door's security chain locked to discourage retorts and spoke as a lecturer, albeit a half-asleep one. "I believe they are us. Our bodies anchor our essence, our soul if you prefer, to this world. When we die, our anchor is lost, and our essence is freed. It leaves this world and enters another. There, it reunites with people who died before us, hence the loved ones often seen during near-death experiences. Ghosts are essences of people who stay nearby or try to reenter this world. Rarely, sentimental souls cling to what they miss, like family homes and childhood dolls. Sadistic souls, on the other hand, see death as an opportunity to torment others.

"Having lost their anchors, ghosts have no physical presence, no way of interacting with this world," Zeb continued. "They merely cast partial shadows, which is why they appear as flickering, disjointed shades rather than intact opaques. I've said this before: it's also why they can't attack the living. Stymied by their limitations, sadistic souls grow more and more frustrated."

"You're saying a ghostly decapitated head isn't decapitated. It has a body we can't see. And it used to be a person, maybe someone we knew."

"Good example, Na. Yes, that's what I believe. It makes more sense than the alternative, that pieces of people can turn into ghosts, like heads and toes."

"Are there helpful spirits?"

"Guardians who protect us from evil ghosts and other dangers? No. Although protective impulses could motivate people to come back, returning has a cost. Moving from this world to the next after dying is natural; moving from the other world back to this one is unnatural. Any who return are damaged by the transition. That's why ghosts don't behave like thinking, planning people. Even when helping, they are vague or erratic. Pointing is about the most they can do.

"Put yourself in their shoes. You know where you are and that what you see is real. You choose to ignore that and focus your attention on a different place, a realm you don't belong to that you can sort of see if you squint your eyes right. How easily could you navigate that other place? At a minimum, the experience would be confusing."

"Understatement," Na groaned.

"Indeed. Finally, recall that to reenter this world, you have to turn your back on the next. There has to be little there to draw you in. It takes a certain kind of person, a damaged person, to reject a promising new world full of friends who passed on before you."

"Okay . . ." She trailed off.

"Is there anything else?"

"Yeah. No. No."

"Good. Keep your word. Go sleep. You have a checkup in the morning." Zeb promptly closed the door. *Thanks, internet, for teaching us that questions should be answered the split second they spring to mind.* Zeb collapsed and resumed sleeping, untroubled by the midnight conversation with his keen assistant.

29

NURSE GINA MAINTAINED a neutral, clipped style of speech and a matching expression. "Have you been resting your arm?" Her steady, sandy eyes perused Na head to toe.

"As much as I can," Na truthfully declared.

"Good. It will heal faster with rest." Gina tapped her tablet computer. "Have you taken each dose of antibiotics on time?"

"Overall. I know that matters."

"It does. Have you experienced side effects? A rash? Double vision? An upset tummy?"

"Nope." A print of a sullen, solitary man treading through a wheat field hung on the wall. It stimulated feelings of longing and abandonment in Na. The nurse's businesslike conduct discouraged her from asking about the decorator's decision-making process.

"Do you need more pain medication?"

"I'm taking as little as I can. Just enough to keep it from thumping."

Gina tapped the tablet again and put it on the counter, next to containers of sanitized paraphernalia. "I am going to verify your injury's improvement and put something on it. Please remove the sling. You may leave your sleeveless shirt on."

"Okay." Na slipped the sling off and rolled it into a ball. Holding a pair of curved scissors, the nurse floated to Na's side and peeled off the bandage cautiously, layer by layer. Na stared at the print on the wall. She had seen the lesion plenty. Tender prodding followed, accompanied by coldness. A medicinal scent, sharper than the one permeating all hospital hallways, wafted to Na's nose.

"Almost done." Gina dabbed Na's shoulder again.

"How's it look?" Na inquired.

"The edges of the scab have been stretched out of position. It has been moving more than it should."

Na abstained from commenting.

"Remaining relaxed and resisting its habitual use is challenging. Tightening your sling may help. However," the nurse continued, "it is healing and clean. There are no signs of infection." She began rewrapping, pulling the gauze snugly around Na's triceps. "Have you had any unusual sensations, such as tingling, muscle weakness, or numbness?"

"I'm not sure," Na hedged. "Sometimes it feels almost cold, like biting on silverware."

"Should you feel weaker or find yourself unable to do something you could do before, that could indicate a serious complication."

"Oh. Nothing like that."

Gina plucked the wadded sling from Na's hand and strapped it on securely. "What about other symptoms, such as dizziness, fainting, or a loss of coordination?"

"Nope." *Honesty would lead to a hundred questions, and I know what caused it. No more hiking. Problem solved.*

"In that case, you are free to leave. Call immediately if it changes color, starts to swell, or smells bad. And please come again on Friday for a follow-up. Puncture injuries do not always mend neatly."

"I will." Na sincerely vowed to do better. The nurse nodded, swooped up her tablet and tools, and vanished. Na stood and fiddled with the sling, then checked the clock on her phone. "Quick and easy."

The spotless corridor running from the waiting room's swinging double doors to a rear emergency exit was empty and silent. Dawdling, she gazed at the far end where she had regained consciousness nearly a week earlier. A sign hanging from the ceiling, ROOM 6, marked its entrance. Na figured it too was vacant, and imagined small-town clinics were peaceful between flu seasons. A familiar prickly aching arose, telling Na it was time to decompress and catch up on the sleep she had lost the previous night.

She ambled down the hall, nosily checking for hints of other patients as she passed the exam rooms; their doors were ajar. *If I'm the only one here, maybe I should find a new doctor.* "Chok!" a woman's voice yelled out from Na's right.

"Choke dee ka," Na replied routinely. The nurse was nowhere to be seen. Na nudged the door open with her knee. A lone, sixty-ish woman with coarse silver hair and wearing a fresh hospital gown sat in a wheelchair. "Pood Thai dai mai ka?" Na asked, just to be certain.

"Bored!" the pallid, agitated patient barked. "Draw! Chalk!" She lunged forward, grabbed an overbed table, and tried to pull herself up. Instead, the mobile table rolled into her, knocking her backward and lifting the wheelchair's small front wheels off the floor. Na instinctively clutched the table and drew it toward herself. Still clinging to it, the patient and her precariously tilted wheelchair stabilized and returned to a vertical position.

"Thank you," Gina tersely approved. "Excuse me." She brushed past Na and set an armful of mug-sized boxes on the overbed table. "You need to rest your arm. All the same, thank you."

The woman, now tranquil, scowled at Gina. "Chalk?"

"Next. This first." Gina spun the wheelchair around, pointing the patient away from Na. A jagged incision ran from below the woman's shoulder blades and up her neck, then over the bump at the rear of her skull, which had been shaved. A great many surgical staples held the incision closed.

Na gasped and gaped. "What happened?"

The nurse began opening the tops of the small boxes. "I cannot say, other than it is a miracle she survived." She spoke customarily: quick and emotionless. "You see now. A fall could have been fatal."

"Yeah."

"Hollow!" the patient abruptly screamed. "Hollow!"

Is she insulting me? I think she is. Jolted, Na couldn't stop herself.

"What is? Me?"

The placid nurse stayed on task.

"Hole! Hole!" the patient fired.

Aghast, Na turned to leave. "I'm going to rest now."

"Please do," Gina replied. "And if you can, close the door. We will see you in a few days."

Her hand on the knob, Na compassionately told the pitiful patient, "Choke dee ka. Good luck," and shut the door behind her. The pain had worsened. Na gripped her right shoulder and felt a knot. "Definitely time to unwind." She thrust her way through the swinging doors and into the clinic's waiting room, entirely unready to schedule a revisit on Friday.

30

TARYN DOGGEDLY TACKLED Dr. Elmir's request to locate particular past officials, their immediate relatives, or their friends. Upbeat about an atypical task, Taryn blazed through the alphabetized list of names and dates he had emailed that morning. Her resources meant she could identify the pertinent Sarah Johnston and Ed White substantially more easily than he. Per his instructions, she marked dubious leads and promptly moved on to the next name. He hadn't asked her to verify the leads, he'd explained, because he wanted to make first contact.

She sipped a hot mug of Postum and rolled on to RICHARDS, M., ~1970. Stressful days and restless nights had persuaded her to decaffeinate. Busy paperwork like this was more Taryn's speed, as opposed to crisis management. Had she enjoyed intensity, she would have gone into emergency services, like her grandfather and uncle. They had both been volunteer firefighters. Rather, she took after her father and aided Milton's day-to-day operations. Every Hale served the town in some capacity, though no streets bore their names.

City Hall was one of the town's oldest structures. Two stories of dark-red brick with flawless stone scrollwork above and below each window, the small, proud building exuded dependability and fortitude. Milton had preserved few historic buildings as its economy changed; just two resided on public lands. Annual budgets perennially contained full funding for City Hall's upkeep. The foyer, mayor's office, and council chamber took up most of the ground floor. The second floor housed city council offices, archives, and valuable, rarely used items, such as the ceremonial mace. Most council members worked at home, however. City Hall's mineral composition blocked Wi-Fi signals.

The phone intercom on Taryn's tidy, L-shaped desk beeped.

"Taryn. Taryn, I . . ." Herbie Handsom hesitated and grunted with exertion. A mighty bang of wood on wood carried out of his office and echoed into the foyer.

Taryn beeped back at once. "Can I help?" Her eyes fell on the 1990s Batgirl figure that sat on her desk between two crystal butterflies. They were the desk's only adornments, all gifts from her mom.

"No, I—I'll get it. I've got it."

"You sure?" Taryn double-checked.

"Never mind." The intercom clicked off, and hollow metal boomed like a drum.

Two probable explanations leapt to Taryn's mind. One, Herbie was rotating the plaques and frames on his walls again, alternating which of his accomplishments could be easily read from his leather executive seat. Two, an uncooperative hornet had flown indoors. Except during winter, Herbie left a window open so the lawn and garden scents could waft in. Claiming he could discern what month it was from his nose alone was Herbie's way of sounding outdoorsy in a town brimming with true woodsmen.

Accepting his word, Taryn got back to Dr. Elmir's list.

"Hnngh." The thick, richly stained door muffled Herbie's voice. "Rrrrgh. Hng-grrrgh." His off-putting noises were impossible to ignore. *That's not a hornet. Don't tell me he's dragging one of his ostentatious bookcases.*

Virtually certain he was doing exactly that, Taryn sighed and got up. *You need help. Why not ask for it?* She gave a warning knock and cracked the mayor's door. The mayor was out of view, but he had opened a window. "I'm coming in."

The mayor crossly rebuked Taryn's invasion from the corner of his desk. "I've got it!" Trash littered the umber carpet. Herbie had dumped out the plastic wastebasket bag, pulled it over his head, and twisted it tightly around his neck. A tenacious chunk of moist grapefruit peel clung to the transparent sack and squashed into his graying sideburn.

"Are you hyperventilating?" Taryn reached to push him into his chair.

"No!" He shook his head and shooed her away. "Out!"

Imitating an angry teacher, she demanded, "Sit and explain yourself!"

Herbie snatched a decorative brass spindle off his desk. A post-campaign present from a friend, its engraving read, POINT US FORWARD! He waved it at Taryn forbiddingly. "Go away! I'll get it!" He backed around his desk toward the open window.

"Get what? You can't breathe. Give. Me. The. Bag!"

"Fine!" Resentfully, he ripped the sack off and threw it at Taryn. The weight of the grapefruit peel carried it past her shoulder. "I'll dig it out. Dig out every bit." Sneering, he rubbed his chest, turned the spindle around, positioned the point between two fingers on his chest, and jammed it in. The brass shaft pierced deeply, straight through his Egyptian cotton dress shirt and all the way to its base. He pulled it out, wheezed, "Hah! Like that?" and jammed it in again, making a new hole in himself. Straining and spitting, he sucked air in and burbled, "Getting out of here." Stupefied, Taryn watched him sit on the window ledge, duck, and roll backward onto the ground outside.

Taryn sped to the window and leaned out. Herbie, on his back amid azalea bushes, feverishly pulled the spindle out and inserted it back in, again and again, soaking himself in blossoming blood. His victorious smirk riveted Taryn. She had no words as the robust, middle-aged man coagulated into a pasty wax replica of himself. Pedestrians shouted from the sidewalk. Fidgety and shaky, Taryn departed the window and slumped onto the desk.

31

TRUSTY, MALLEABLE RESEARCH subjects were practically irreplaceable. Their reliability meant they were suitable for the most sensitive experiments. Medications and procedures must adhere to predetermined schedules to yield worthwhile results. Skipping treatments invalidated data and squandered costly resources. Missing a session was intolerable. *My deadlines cannot be postponed. Once he is found,* the investigator seethed, *I will offset these losses by withholding palliatives.*

The investigator's car smoothly coasted to a halt in the subject's short driveway. Shrubs and young trees created a natural fence between the main road and the white house's front yard. Casual passersby would not catch the investigator snooping unless they were on foot. Neighbors were another story. They could rear their heads at any moment. The investigator got out and, in spite of the fury hammering through his limbs, gently eased the car door closed. *Did you forget I know where you live? Snubbing my messages will not keep you hidden.*

The morning sun was too bright to see inside the house from the driveway; its indoor lights could have been on or off. No smoke rose from the chimney, not that there should have been a fire today. Promisingly, it was definitely the subject's coupe in the carport attached to the right side of the house. The investigator hopped onto the porch, gave an authoritarian knock, and listened. He heard only ambient chirping. The doorbell was equally fruitless. He knocked and rang one more time: not a scuffle. He rattled the knob: locked. He lifted the doormat: nothing. "Gah!"

The investigator could tell the small house had been well maintained once. Its front lawn had manicured edges, and empty flower beds ringed the property all the way to the rear of the residence. Currently untended, the yard had grown rough. Weeds had crept in, beauty bark had rotted, and patches of small rocks indicated where raindrops had eroded the garden's topsoil. A rake and shovel leaned against the left side of the house, next to a vertically standing wheelbarrow and a rusted charcoal grill filthy with gummy ash. Fresh footprints, the investigator surmised, would not look out of place along there. He furtively moved to the backyard.

The rear of the house had been abandoned long before the front. Blotched with daisies and moss, the lawn was no longer a lawn. In the near corner of the yard, the investigator passed exposed cement blocks housing metal anchors which had probably secured a swing set long ago. The basic back door had a small shingled awning and two steps. It was locked too, but its knob was loose. Hoping for a push-button lock on the other side, the investigator gave the knob a hearty jiggle. Its button obligingly popped out and permitted the investigator to sidle inside.

He had not visited the subject's home before, but this was not a social call. The investigator disregarded its bleak interior design and swiftly ducked into each room, carefully keeping his hands to himself. A short hall led from the kitchen and living room, where the external doors were, to a moderate bathroom, two unoccupied bedrooms, and a master bedroom. He discovered his missing subject in the master bedroom, half covered by blankets, dead and cold to the touch. *Good. You didn't run.*

The investigator counted his options. Complete carcass disposal required finding every single medication, receipt, schedule, and appointment reminder so the investigator wouldn't be suspected of disappearing the subject. An accidental house fire could be staged, but the subject was not a smoker. Fire fatalities not attributable to smoking were inherently suspicious. If not disposed of, the body had to maintain its current pose due to lividity. The subject could be moved to the bathtub and left to soak, but if found too soon, its lividity wouldn't be a perfect match to its pose. A conscientious forensic pathologist would spot the inconsistency and report that the scene had been tampered with.

Finally, the investigator could do nothing and walk away, trusting the neighbors had not seen him. Every option that eliminated evidence would bring greater scrutiny and interference. The investigator wrinkled his nose. *Messy. I will not fall prey to this trap.* He elected to walk away and rely on his prior precautions to shield himself from law enforcement's eyeballs and subsequent research interruptions.

Before exiting, he stood at the subject's footboard and briefly reminisced. The man had been an exemplary participant. *Impending death is why we reach for meaning and purpose. We want to be valued. Having value, we can cope with mortality. Nearly incapacitated by your fear of death, you strove for flawless obedience and provided an unanticipated opportunity.* The subject had precisely followed instructions at the tiniest implication of an impossible recuperation from his amputation. But his death defeated his purpose.

You lost your value. You wasted my time. Someone else will be the bridge that substantiates my methods. You die what you were when we met: worthless. Let the cards fall where they will. I will succeed. Your death will not stop me.

32

"THE CITY COUNCIL appointed Dad interim mayor last night. He and I need your help."

Boone gravely nodded in assent.

"It's horrific." Gathered around a small table in a deserted council member's office with Taryn, Boone, and Na, Zeb leaned forward and rested his forearms on its edge. "Would you like to talk, Taryn?"

She lowered her puffy eyes. "I'm . . . not ready. For this"—she patted a vibrant-blue hanging folder on the table—"I am. Dad?"

"No, no, I'm just here to legitimize the meeting. This is your show." Even in this subdued setting, Boone possessed an uplifting magnetism. Zeb reckoned that was why Na spoke highly of him.

"Alright." Taryn skimmed her phone. "Dr. Elmir, your university bio says you specialize in the supernatural?"

"Past and present cultural and psychological studies that include paranormal aspects, yes."

"Have you met Wade Havelock? Do you know his version of the plant accident?"

"Yes," Zeb plainly affirmed. He had not disclosed to the mayor that Wade was his primary contact.

"Until this morning, I didn't. Herbie collated the final report himself and excluded Mr. Havelock's account entirely."

"Most would have done the same."

"Me too," Taryn verified, "until yesterday. Herbie wo— It wasn't natural." Her voice cracked and rose. "Someone got him. He was tricked or poisoned or, I don't know, hypnotized? I searched his desk for who might've done it and what else he'd hidden from me."

Zeb scratched his leg. "I'm sorry. Truly, I don't mean to press, but can you clarify 'not natural'?"

Na quickly turned toward Zeb and spoke, more to him than Taryn. "You can trust us. We won't criticize you."

"What he did. His behavior." She closed her eyes. Boone squeezed her arm. "He was fine. Everyday Herbie. Then he's stabbing himself, saying, 'I'll get it.' He fell outside and didn't stop. He stabbed until . . . No one does that."

"I'm sorry I had to ask. Thank you." Zeb gave Na a knowing look. *He did it to himself.*

Na brushed off his gaze, scooted closer to Taryn, and widened her eyes. "Do you know what he meant? Could you see what 'it' was?"

"There was nothing to see." Crestfallen, Na slouched onto the table. Taryn continued, "But that's my question: Wade. Dr. Elmir, why do people see ghosts?"

"Well, three potential reasons. One, misfiring neurons somewhere in our nervous systems. Two, our brains misinterpreting sensations we can't consciously identify, such as dusty sunbeams. Three, glimpsing residual energy left behind by trauma, like a scar or imprint on reality. I have my own theories but don't want to digress."

"Drugs cause hallucinations. Illnesses too," Boone added.

"That's correct, yes, as can grief. There are many potential reasons," Zeb reiterated.

"It would be pointless to search for causes, in other words," Taryn brooded. "But what about motives? What if Herbie and Wade were targeted?"

"You're guessing they're linked?" Zeb's wording earned a disapproving scowl from Na.

"Herbie sent Chief Rawls to interview someone." Taryn pulled a police incident report out of the folder. "Either Herbie had a suspect or he was open to Mr. Havelock's account. Chief Rawls didn't find anything, but that's what this folder is: everything Herbie had on Jackson Mender and Mender's Nursery. Herbie fiercely defended Milton's image to a fault but directed me to aid your research. My intuition says he planned to give it to you."

"Like I told Na"—Boone grimaced—"it's abnormal. This isn't Milton. I'd be mad if Herbie hadn't been alarmed."

Na perked up. "A garden store? Has it been open long?"

"More than eight years." Boone patted his sternum. "Old enough for grudges. The name's a metaphor. They teach meditation. Nondenominational and a-religious, they say, but they're far out enough that our more traditional citizens eschew it. They're supposedly friendly. They wouldn't spurn your inquiries, I don't think."

"You haven't heard of it," Taryn correctly presumed. "You've been reading official records and statements; Mender's wouldn't come up. It's a Milton oddity. A few locals fear it, but it has followers and attracts 'spiritual tourists,' you might say. Herbie had nothing against them, as far as I know. He accepted anybody who draws folks to town, including Jackson Mender. But he could detect others' intentions. If he suspected Mender's . . . It's within your study, right? Could you see if they're involved? Not just with the factory, but Herbie too."

"It may fall within our purview," Zeb equivocated. "What about the other victim, Davis Thomason? Was his testimony in the final report?"

"We need his therapist's permission to get it. The accident disturbed him, on top of losing his hand. But the OSHA report had a deadline, so the idea was to tack it on as an addendum."

"Do you know his condition? Is it PTSD? Agoraphobia?"

"No. His therapist is tight lipped. We don't know why he got hurt, either. Did Mr. Havelock bump him? Did they fight? Was his attention on Wade and the rest when he got caught in the machine? The report said Wade Havelock's the culprit, but the first aid he gave probably saved Davis's life. Davis was basically catatonic in the hospital; they couldn't get much out of him."

That's why he hasn't called back. One mystery solved. "Well, I could visit Mender disguised as an interested outsider. However, it's likely a dead end. His nursery is an obvious starting point for an investigation that's spinning its wheels. The New Age movement hasn't brought an eruption of hauntings. Neither would a meditation center. This—I mean, the factory accident—had a different instigator."

"Let me go. I'll pretend to be a customer. He'll be less guarded against a customer." Na pinched a corner of the blue folder to stake a claim on it.

"Arm and all?" Zeb deliberated. *It would be unquestionably better than her stewing in the hotel, and I'm not done calling those people Taryn tracked down.*

"I won't go by myself. Doug will come. He owes me, and if it's an oddity, he should know about it already."

"Doug from Stuffs? You've seen him since our first day here?" Zeb realized that Na must have spent her free time doing more than vegetating and asked himself why that hadn't occurred to him sooner.

"A couple times. Stuffs is convenient. Please," Na begged the table, "let me contribute."

"Mmmm," Taryn mulled. "It's your decision, Dr. Elmir."

Zeb extended Na's suspense. "Convince me, Na. Do you know what to ask, what to watch for?"

"Well enough, and I'll study the folder. It's not like my going would burn bridges. If you're not satisfied, go yourself without me."

"Persuasive points. You win." Zeb smirked. "Call or text him or whatever. See how soon Doug can go."

"I'll drop by his shop. He should be working."

"Well, you're officially authorized by the interim, figurehead mayor," Boone quipped. "If you need anything, ask Taryn, and she'll take care of you."

"Be careful, Na."

"I will, Taryn. I swear."

33

"**DON'T TELL ME** you came for the food," Wade lightheartedly accused. "Today's chicken cacciatore and stewed root vegetables."

"Of course not." Zeb's informal solid gray socks matched his manner. "How are you?"

"Fair to middling. It's weird. When I'm better, stress kicks in. And I can't do anything about it. I can't look for a job, can't swing by the pub. I gotta stay cooped up and tough it out. It's worse than being bedridden, except for the 'thinking I'm about to die' part." Wade semifacetiously grinned from his kitchen.

"You know you can call anytime you're bored. It's the least I can do." Zeb leaned his laptop, still in its carrying case, on the floor against the side of his chair.

"If you say so, boss."

"How have you been sleeping?"

Wade stirred a pot with a large wooden spoon, then joined Zeb in the living room. "Normal, maybe?"

"You're having nightmares." Zeb almost reached for his laptop, then reconsidered.

"Once or twice a night. Not bad. I fall back to sleep pretty quick."

"Do the dreams stay with you after waking up?"

"It's kind of the other way around. Life stays with me when I sleep, if you take my meaning."

Zeb did. "Nightmares are, for lack of a better word, expected."

"Yup, 'expected' fits."

"And when you're awake, sense anything strange? Get the heebie-jeebies?"

"Not since. You must've been right. They're not hunting me."

"What about close friends or family? Have you talked with them?"

"My older sister's a great ear, but she can't digest my jabbering. She's a down-to-earth type and doesn't understand what I'm talking about. It's all good, though. I know she's there when I need to vent."

"Can she come stay to keep you company?"

"Nah, she's out of state, like the rest of my family. And having a friend over's a bad idea. I'm particular in certain respects," he chuckled with self-awareness. "My friendships might not survive a sleepover. Do you *know* how people handle their toothbrushes?"

"Changing topics, did you hear about Mayor Handsom?"

"Yeah." Wade shook his head. "I liked him. He was cheerful, not one of those fear-ramming 'this town's in the toilet' politicians."

"After the accident, did he contact you, directly or indirectly?"

"Indirectly?"

"Through someone else, via his staff or the police. Did he ever ask you about what happened, or your health or hobbies, or anything like that?"

"No. No one but company reps, you, and my family have talked about it since I gave the police my statement. None of my old coworkers have called—kind of hurtful, honestly. I figure the owners told them not to, to control the story. If the plant's haunted, who's going to stay, am I right?"

"But nothing from the mayor," Zeb repeated, "not an email or phone message?"

"Zippo. Why?"

"He was being more thorough than I had thought, is all. The official reports were finished, but something about your case weighed on him."

"That's no conundrum. His stepfather owns the factory. He was watching out for his family."

34

NA SWUNG THE door and jingled its chimes with fanfare before strolling into Stuffs. The store was empty again. *Feast or famine*, she thought. *Retail life.*

"It's you," Doug belched.

"It's me. Yay?" Na eyed Doug to get a bead on his state. He had a conspicuously dispirited aura as he sat on a stool behind the counter, hunched over a spread of papers. He breathed through his mouth and wrote slowly, twitching his cheek as he shifted from one paper to the next. "You look like you're studying grammar."

"S-sorry." Doug stacked his forms and leapt to attention. "How's your arm? Want mints?"

"I need a favor. And info." Fully stocked backpack in hand, Na marched forward. "What can you tell me about Mender's Nursery?"

"Mender's? That marble cult?"

"Did you say 'marble cult'? They worship marbles?"

"Uh, it's what I heard they do. My parents said to stay away, and I have."

"As a big boy with his own store," Na goaded, "would they let you go now?"

Doug impassively retorted, "They died three years ago. A tree fell on their car. This was their shop."

"Shit. Sorry."

"That floating head . . . Grassoo?"

"Krasue."

"Krasue. If ghosts are real, there *must* be life after death."

Na went with the flow and moved on from her misstep. "Ugh,

I'm turning into Dr. Elmir. It depends on what ghosts are. Dr. Elmir believes there is, I think."

"You?"

"Conflicted. I want it both ways. An afterlife would be a positive for those we love."

Doug twirled and fumbled his pen. "The thought makes seeing that nasty wad worth it."

"Yes. On the other hand, it's not all roses. If Dr. Elmir is right, evil people get afterlives too. Evil people would stay evil after dying. Or get evil-er. But he believes we're safe, that the dead can't hurt us. According to Dr. Elmir, Krasue wasn't a threat."

"What a load," Doug scoffed.

"Half a load. If he's wrong about being safe, what could living people do against murderous ghosts? We couldn't arrest or imprison them. We'd be defenseless and knee-deep in victims. He has to be wrong, but he can't be totally wrong. We're missing a piece." *Although . . .* "Anyway, you're the expert. What about the marble cult?"

"They have a big marble and have meetings to worship it."

"A special marble?"

"Dunno."

"And?"

"Mender is super skinny. Like, 'see his bumpy bones through his skin' skinny."

Her left arm akimbo, Na rattled off, "He's single, thirty-nine, from South Dakota, and got a massage degree from a diploma mill. He's been arrested five times protesting for animal rights and has two traffic tickets for driving too slowly."

"Wow. You've been digging."

"That's honestly all you know? Including rumors?"

"I can drive there," Doug sheepishly submitted.

"Hey, you're not useless! We're paying them a visit. Undercover. I'm your friend. I want alternatives to pain pills because of a classmate who got addicted to opioids. You heard they teach meditation and suggested trying it."

"Wait, undercover?"

"For science!"

"Your study?"

"It's a unique part of the local culture. We'll just give it a quick peek, see if it deserves a deep dive. I don't want a commotion. For an authentic snapshot of what the marble means to them, we have to be undercover." Na stopped short of the potential danger. *If it's a dead end like Dr. Elmir said, it'd be cruel to make Doug worry two days after Krasue. Doug seems jumpy about Mender's anyway.*

"Alright. But you're the one in a sling, so you can ask anything. I'm from here. If they recognize me, I need an excuse for why the 'Stuffs kid' is snooping. We should be dating. That'll explain me asking a bunch of questions. I'm being caring and protective. It'll keep things from getting weird, too."

"Weird how?"

"Flirting."

"Who's going to flirt?" Na asked incredulously. "Not Mender."

"Anyone," Doug hemmed. "When do you want to go?"

"Can you close up and go now?"

"I *can* . . ."

"Will you?"

"I can't say no, can I?"

Na brightly replied, "Not while preserving your honor."

"Okay, gimme a sec."

"Grab a box of mints for the road."

"It's like a six-minute drive."

"Better grab three," Na teased.

35

A LOCKED DRIVEWAY gate forced Doug to park on the road's shoulder. They left Doug's blue pickup and sauntered up a dirt footpath, past the gate and a wooden MENDER'S NURSERY: OPEN sign. Another, larger sign stood a few feet onto the property. White with black hand lettering and colorfully painted flowers, it read:

Kindness Please
- *No shaming*
- *No cussing*
- *No scowling*
- *No recording*
- *No selling*
- *Casual nudity*

"Fair warning is fair request," Doug remarked.

The driveway, also dirt, ran parallel to the path. Both curled through a grassy field infinitely more benevolent than the dentist's. Long emerald leaves rasped peacefully in a breeze. Na missed the beach. She kept the sentiment to herself. "It's made for meditating."

"Probably an old farm," Doug speculated. A group of four gorgeous, reddish-brown animals grazed out in the field. The tops of their heads were black, and one had thick horns that curved backward. They pranced together peppily, childlike and oblivious. "Cool! Oberhasli goats!"

Na raised an eyebrow. "Oberhasli?"

"Would you believe my cousin works at a livestock supply store?"

"Mm-mm. Rejected. Weak justification you copied from a TV drama."

"But less embarrassing than 'I watch gobs of goat videos.'"

"Not judging." Na waved him off. "Screaming goats are hilarious."

Further up the path, just past an ancient tree with many branches, a broad concrete birdbath stood next to a pedestal supporting a medium-sized wooden chest. There was another painted sign, smaller than the first: TAKE A PAPER AND HOLD IT. IMAGINE WRITING DOWN TODAY'S STRESSORS, FEARS, AND AGITATIONS. PLACE YOUR PAPER IN THE WATER. NOT REQUIRED. ONLY YOU WILL KNOW IF YOU DON'T.

"Let's play along." Na opened the chest's hinged lid, took out two sheets of thin paper, and handed one to Doug. "It's translucent. Tissue paper?" *I could fill both sides*, Na thought.

Doug smiled empathically. "This might take a while."

A few moments later, Na held her sheet over the center of the birdbath and dropped it in. It curled in the water and dissolved into nothing. "Neat! Ahhh, this is why he makes guests park on the road."

"Marketing," Doug derided.

"C'mon, get in the mood. We *want* to be here, remember? You're taking care of your girlfriend."

"Right, right." Doug plopped his sheet into the birdbath. "I wrote my preconceptions about this place."

"I wrote about you."

"Naturally. We *are* a couple."

"We are." Na nabbed his flaccid hand in hers. "Let's go."

The path led up a soft grade to an expanse of rough lawn scattered with fruit trees. The driveway ended at a taupe, respectably clean mobile home. A pool of crushed seashells formed a patio surface. To their right was a spacious clearing, occupied by conical, hemp-canvas tents encircling a large marble sphere. White with gray ribboning, the sphere was at least as tall as Na and glittered in the sun. Na couldn't guesstimate how much it weighed.

Doug paused for Na to make the first move. "House or tents?"

Na led. "Orb-ward we go." She released Doug and skipped ahead to rub both hands on the smooth marble. "Touch it! It's cold!"

A tawny-haired man with a ducktail beard bobbed out of a tent. Shirtless and in green corduroy shorts, he had a marathoner's frame and tan skin. His breathy voice chanted, "Planet reminds us how we should be. Blessings."

"Hello. I'm Doug. Are you Mr. Mender?"

"I am Jackie. Welcome to my nursery. What services do you seek?"

"My girlfriend's hurt bad, and she can't take pills forever; it's unhealthy." Doug stuck to Na's script. "I think meditation might be safer. The meditation you teach, can it replace drugs?"

"Hello. I'm Na."

Jackie bowed to Na. "Yes. A right mind can learn."

"She's in, like, nonstop agony. How long does your training take?"

"Short or long. The mind decides." Jackie joined Na and stroked the sphere as if it were a horse. "We gather to share our peacefulness. In inclement weather, the tents shelter us. The tents aid new students who desire solitude, as well. Together, we accept nature and our roles within it. Acceptance removes the cages and barricades materialism foists upon us. We are what we are. In being what we are, we set free discomfiting thoughts of what we are not. This teaches our minds to fearlessly feel. No dread. No anger. No accusation. No regret. The power of pain is sapped. What remains is more easily tended."

"Erm, that sounds expensive," Doug grumbled sincerely.

Jackie's reply was unperturbed. "You alone know the value of your experience at the nursery, and there exist multiple means of gifting. You decide which gifts of thankfulness are suitable to provide."

Shocked, Doug blurted, "Your classes are free?"

"Their value lies within you. Should they have no value, give no gift."

Na rejoined Doug and reclasped his hand. "When is today's class?"

"Today is inauspicious. The nursery requests nursing. Tomorrow at three we shall hold fellowship. If you attend and are able to withstand, do not medicate after one. Pure minds and bodies meditate best."

"Got it," Na pledged. Her arm had been twinge-free today. *Perhaps tomorrow,* she contemplated, *I could be wholly drug-free—* except for the antibiotics preventing gangrene in her puncture. "Should we bring mats or towels?"

"Willing minds are enough. And before I forget, please let our goat friends mellow in the meadow as you leave."

Na elbowed Doug and said, "Your Oberhaslis are beautiful."

"They are not *mine*, but I agree. They emanate . . . dignity. Farewell."

Na and Doug retreated down the path. Beyond the birdbath and completely out of earshot, Na shared her impression of the guru. "He's, like, too stereotypical. Cartoony."

"More marketing. People have to think his nursery is unique to donate money. And if his students feel like he's given them something, they're obliged to give back."

"I can't believe anybody would buy that act. He didn't strike me as sinister, though."

"Yeah. He's more of a hipster hippie than a witch doctor. Did you have a hunch he'd be sinister?"

Na thought Doug was still shaken from Krasue and didn't want to overwhelm him with what Taryn had said. *What you don't know can't hurt you.* "Oh, I mean he's not selling spells, potions, and hexes. He won't send specters to haunt his clients' targets."

"Yeah. Although, I get why Mom and Dad told me to keep away. He's not, um, conventionally holy."

"Dr. Elmir and I knew it would be a dead end." Finally past the gate and on the road, Na let go of Doug's hand. "When he said '*goat friend*,' was it two words or one? Having a goat friend is okay, but a *goatfriend* is less okay. 'Hey, Mom, I want you to meet my goatfriend.' 'I met my goatfriend at the petting zoo.' 'My goatfriend has a kid.'"

"Two words; it had to be two words. Shudder. We have to go back, don't we?" Doug unlocked his truck.

"We can't quit prematurely no matter how dead the end is. The class will be definitive, and we'll scope out his customers. Like, he could have taught spirit manipulation to the wrong person." Na climbed inside and fished in her backpack, which she had left underneath the seat. "Don't start the truck yet. I need a favor."

"Anything."

She tapped her phone on and passed it to Doug. "There's video from the night you rescued me. The idea of watching it makes me sick, but I have to know what's on it. Will you watch it?"

"Ugh, I don't know," he queasily replied.

Na urged, "I shouldn't be on it. And I turned the sound off. I don't want to hear me scream either."

"I should look for the lumberjack, right? See if he showed?"

"Exactly. Or anything else, um, Krasue-y."

"Ughhh." Doug hovered his finger over the phone, hesitated, and clicked play. "It's messier in there than I remember." Unflinching at first, Doug's face contorted and settled into relief. "Nothing. It's dirty and dark and then the phone goes flying."

Wonderful. The story's a bust, and I'm hurt for nothing. Na snatched her phone, deleted the video, and zipped it into her bag. "Let's head home. I'll meet you at Stuffs after two tomorrow."

"As you wish."

36

"BECAUSE MATTER LIVES, our guest lives. A doctor might say, 'No pulse. No movement. It does not eat or grow. It is dead. Inanimate.' We know better! Planet will move and grow. It will become innumerable components that fuse with others into new organisms: a grasshopper, a zucchini, an infant. And these new organisms will move and grow and become innumerable components that fuse again! Matter is life. It is all life that has been and will be. Matter wants to become. It *desires* to become, and so it does eternally, unceasingly, becoming one thing and then the next. It desires! It lives!

"This living universe loses nothing. Matter becomes energy, and energy becomes matter. All of us, all lives, are matter and energy made of the components of others' matter and energy. And our bodies are physical structures designed to transmit energy. Life transmits energy in patterns. Our memories, our emotions, our movements, our relationships are nerves shooting electrical messages to other nerves. When I touch you and you touch me, we share energy. We share patterns. We become one structure, one circuit transmitting electricity, yet we remain us. *We remain us.* Our energy patterns are always ours. We unite and separate and alter positions and forms and reunite. Through it all, we are us.

"And we falter. We tangle into unhealthy patterns, unhealthy thoughts and actions. Unhealthy patterns are transmitted to lives surrounding us. They receive our transmissions and are changed negatively. We disrupt their patterns, their health. And it is our fault, for we remain us. Our patterns are ours. The patterns we transmit are our responsibility. We have a duty to accept ourselves, to love and be aware of ourselves and admit our dignity. It is not selfish to do so. It is responsible. For when we do, we are healthy and so are our transmissions. We pass our health outward, healing and strengthening surrounding lives and repairing the damage we do when we are tangled."

Jackie's rambling, mood-setting sermon depleted Na's self-restraint, but her peers were enthralled. Thirteen attentive thirty-something-and-over women attended the class with Na and Doug. They were all cushion-carrying disciples, dressed in either workout clothes or robes. Jackie had greeted each by name upon their arrival, and each had poutily smiled back. In unpunished violations of Jackie's third rule, a few had also frowned at their classmates. His clan had not attained perfect harmony.

"Therefore, meditate on the Planet. It is what it is: peacefulness, tranquility, acceptance. Allow your own patterns to be. Allow you to be you. In downpouring rain, in dusklight, in frost, the stone is marble. The marble is itself. You be you.

"Now divide and meditate on yourself as the Planet. We have two new pupils. Please defer tents to them and share the rest according to modesty. Should your meditations struggle, turn your palms upward, and I will provide consult. Dignity and blessings."

"Dignity and blessings," the class unanimously repeated before fanning out.

"So much to say," Doug whispered. "Like, how Dad would have reacted if Mom socialized with a shirtless dude in a hut."

"Shh, he's coming!"

"May I guide you to your tents?" Jackie extended his arms. "Isolation is recommended. Because you are a couple, you will be opposites, facing the Planet and each other in spiritual counterbalance."

No choice, Na thought with resignation. "That's fine. Whatever you advise."

"Can't we share a tent?"

"Alas, our tents are singles to promote meditation."

Doug feebly objected, "Her arm. She might—"

Na addressed Doug, then Jackie, "It's fine. It's fine."

"I don't like it."

"Come." Jackie ushered them to a white tent nearby. He unzipped the vertical entrance and lifted one of its triangular flaps. Motioning with a cloth tie attached to the flap, Jackie asked Doug, "Open or closed?"

"Open," Doug responded glumly.

Jackie rolled up the flap and tied it in place. "There you are." He gestured like a restaurant waiter treating his customers to a sought-after booth. Doug shuffled inside and crossed his legs. Jackie gave him a priestly farewell bow and led Na around the marble sphere to an identical tent.

"Closed," Na told him before Jackie could ask. The sphere completely blocked her view of Doug; leaving herself visible only had disadvantages. She delicately clambered into the compartment.

"Very good. I shall leave it unzipped and loose for easy egress. Turn your palms upward for assistance. There is no shame in Mender's Nursery. Only discovery." Jackie disappeared behind the floppy canvas and walked away.

Na folded her legs in the lotus position and pondered what to do. The bare, remarkably clean tent suited meditation. Its fibrous fabric walls softened sunlight to a sleepy Saturday morning. Without a cushion, the ground was firm but not unpleasantly hard. Na had room to stretch her legs if they went numb, but as Jackie had said, two occupants would be cramped. Whatever else he was behind, Jackie at least cared about his students.

What *was* Jackie behind? From the get-go, the nursery had carried a benign vibe. Granted a tad shifty, Jackie himself radiated no cruelty. An ongoing plot to terrorize and cull Milton's citizenry seemed beyond him. But he was fishy: his life revolved around a boulder, animal husbandry, and relaxing. It was too shallow. There had to be more to Jackson Mender.

Anyhow, Na had heeded Jackie and abstained from drugs all day. She expected stinging and vertigo, and maybe fainting, as the drugs flushed out of her system. Instead, her marred muscle had been prickle-free with a mere background soreness she had no trouble ignoring. If the drugs did nothing to quell the prickling, could it be a warning symptom of another condition? The doctor had mentioned nerve damage.

Recalling that pain, Na rocked on her haunches, back and forth. Every instance of that pain had knocked her virtually unconscious and drowned her in nightmarish imagery. With no one to describe the episodes to, Na had suppressed her worries about their significance.

Na heard hushed muttering outside and froze mid-rock. Jackie and a woman pattered inaudibly. Fractionally louder, Jackie reassuringly stated, "Happily. No blame. No guilt. Nature made us thus." Loud shuffling and a minute of silence proceeded. Na's undercover role mandated she keep eavesdropping. The woman moaned. "Slower. Ah, oh. Oh, oh-ahh-ahhhh." He soothed her: "We are all beautiful. Embrace your beauty."

Actual meditation rookies would want coaching, but Doug wouldn't have the wherewithal to ask. Na had to bite the bullet. It was fine. After all, she was ostensibly the reason they had come. She stoically closed her eyes, breathed deeply, displayed her clammy palms, and recited a mantra: *I don't know what I just heard. I don't know what I heard.*

Hand sanitizer wafted into her tent. Jackie lilted to Na, "You have questions, yes? How may I assist?"

"Yes." Na wiped her eyes and gathered herself. "Well, I get how meditating helps stress, but when the pain zings, I double over. What am I supposed to do then?"

"Stay afloat. Don't sink. Accept the pain and set it free. Do not dwell on it or ruminate. Do not fret. Acknowledge and release it. The very moment pain ceases, it is out of your thoughts. Do this with stress, and you can do so with rage and pain. You will hurt, but only when you are hurting. Not before, not after."

"It's managing my reaction, not the pain itself."

"Muscle cramps, headaches—for these, the pain itself. For injuries, your reactions."

"How long have you taught? Have there been many patients like me?"

"Most want emotional respite. Some bring corporeal complaints. A few like you have come in my years. For all, the mind decides. Resistant minds who quarrel cannot align with the Planet."

"Oh, of course." Na feigned understanding. "Do you give intensive classes for special situations?"

"This is all I donate. I replenish myself between sessions. I must, to aid my pupils."

"Do men attend your classes?"

"Seldomly. Narrow views of masculinity mistakenly label meditation 'feminine.' A sadness. In truth, balance has no gender."

"How about metaphysical counseling?"

"Ah, transcendental. A perilous route." Jackie's serene demeanor was unfazed. "My humble gifts are insufficient; my talent is the physical plane."

"Perilous?"

Jackie mimed a tipping scale with his hands. "Modern activity tangles the mind. Meditation unties, rebalances. Our weighty Planet grants us colossal inspiration, restoring equilibrium. Yet our Planet's gargantuan mass cannot unravel or rebalance transcendental knots. Knots of the kind strangle and dominate. They," Jackie sighed, "are inoperable."

"Interesting. Okay then. Thanks." Na reset her posture to shoo him away. Jackie withdrew and reclosed the fabric flaps.

Alone and cognizant of why they had come, Na stayed alert by muting her phone and playing a free puzzle app. She was immune to the temptation of microtransactions and switched games whenever the advertising became overly aggressive. Her enjoyment came from basic self-satisfaction and mild mental exercise, not unlocking bonuses or competing for global rankings. The pleasing distraction kept her flicking and tapping her finger for the duration of their session.

A resonant ting preceded an announcement from Jackie. "Peaceful egress, compatriots, peaceful egress." He tinged the chimes again.

Is he pompous or just artificial? Na crawled outside and gradually stood as she readjusted to daylight. Her classmates were already huddled by their guru, a gardener in a plot of strawberries.

Doug nervously burst around the marble. "This guy's a loon. You alright? Did he bother you?"

"Hi. No. Yes."

"What?!" Doug confrontationally spun in Jackie's direction.

"No, I'm fine. Don't talk; I don't want to linger. Let's slip out while Jackie's engulfed in admirers. We should report to Dr. Elmir. Let's tell him everything. *Everything* everything."

37

DUMBFOUNDED BY THEIR original report, Zeb had Na and Doug restart at the beginning of their burn pit and Nursery adventures. He treated them as primary witnesses and video-recorded their complete chronicles on his laptop without comment, interrupting only for clarifying confirmations and explicit details. Doug kept his hands in his pockets, spoke succinctly, and frequently looked at Na as if seeking approval to reveal their shared secrets. Na was forthright and animated, a paradigm of conviction, until she began describing her injury's side effects. That's when her saga lost momentum and wavered.

"How I'm blacking out from pain . . . what I saw when I fainted—sorry I lied, Doug. I haven't told anyone. Not the doctor either. Was what I saw real, Dr. Elmir? Did a ghost claw at me and turn into Krasue?"

"Back up, Na. What happened when you fainted, step by step?"

"My arm prickled, like when a bee lands on your face and walks on your eyelid. A sticky prickle. That turned into pain. I couldn't think and passed out. That's when I saw the ghosts. They saw me back. One tried to get me, but Doug called and woke me up. And Krasue was right there."

"Ah. Good news." Zeb clapped. "People can dream during syncope—fainting. Coming out of syncope isn't instantaneous. Some mental functions activate before others, meaning you can perceive things in your vicinity and unknowingly incorporate them into a dream. For instance, you might awaken from slumber and notice a coat hanging from a hall tree. From that coat, your half-awake mind could generate nightmares about a kidnapper standing over you. It's possible that you would not be able to separate your real perceptions from details you dreamt and would eventually believe wholeheartedly that a home invader had tried to abduct you.

"In short, Na, you're not one hundred percent. You're brittle. Overexertion brings pain, which knocks you out. While unconscious, you dream. It's common. Just don't start telling people you were kidnapped while working as my assistant."

Na and Doug duetted, "Really!?"

"Jinx," Doug grunted.

"Now stop overexerting yourself," Zeb admonished, "and tell me if you faint again so we can get you back to the doctor."

"I'm seeing him tomorrow. You're *how* sure I dreamt it?"

"Ninety-five percent. Mathematical certainty. I estimate you two encountered a wraith, which is what triggered your dream. It fit Krasue's visual description, but understand, Krasue's description is folklore, a set of beliefs accumulated over generations. It's not factual or encyclopedic. Although you hobbled, it poofed before you reached Doug's truck. Hardly the relentless predator depicted in the myths."

Is this conversion disorder? Zeb wondered. *Are their interactions inducing ailments and hallucinations, bringing their fears to life?* Wade, a patient rebounding from life-threatening pneumonia, was certainly a conversion disorder risk. As was Rojana. She'd been exposed to a gaggle of distressing life events, which have evidently been relayed to her devoted partner. In turn, this poor fellow had become susceptible too. *Or is something, either here or hereafter, driving Milton's spirits to prowl?* Humans were complex but typically had simple motivations. Ghosts, in their warped states, were simpler. *What could rile them up? Conversion disorder is statistically more common than rioting undead. Nonetheless, hmm.*

"I'm confused." Doug massaged his left thigh with his palm. "Did it paralyze me? Something did."

"That's normal too. You froze." *Or you have conversion disorder.* But he couldn't say that, because trying to talk people out of it was fruitless. "Don't be embarrassed. Freezing is a basic response to stress that has nothing to do with your mindset or personality. It doesn't mean you're weak or not macho or that you'll freeze again in the future. It doesn't make you cowardly. This one time you were threatened, your body locked up. It can happen to anyone at any time, and it's more likely in extreme circumstances. Seeing a ghost for the first time, especially a Krasue, counts as extreme. That was your first time, right?"

"Yeah, I woulda mentioned if not."

"And you're the sort of guy who explores the wilderness at night. Seriously, don't sweat it."

Doug returned his hand to his pocket. "Got it."

"Krasue or not, it was wise to run. You can't unsee a ghoul like that. There was no point in memorizing every detail." Na and Doug's poses still broadcast tension. "Are there any details you omitted? What sensations you felt?"

They eyed each other and shrugged.

"How about déjà vu, like you were reenacting a play?"

"Definitely not," Na declared.

I tried. They're not in a receptive mood. "We can talk more later. Let's call it a day and think about what we want to do next. That includes you, Doug. Consider what you need going forward. I want to help."

"Uh-kay," Doug droned like a freshman receiving a homework assignment.

Mender's was a bust. They've bonded, fed into each other. I may have erred. But she was warned. At any rate, more data is more data. Tomorrow I'll see where it takes me.

38

NA FASTENED HER seat belt and said, "Thanks for picking me up."

"Aww, what's another day. I hardly get morning customers. The rush isn't till school's out. We'll be back this afternoon, right?"

"I would think." *Not a lie. There's a chance we will.* She didn't like taking advantage of his generosity, but there was no choice. And he took pride in his hometown knowledge; if she pushed him away, he'd insist on helping—possibly out of guilt too, even though it wasn't his fault. *Yeah, asking could offend him. It's better not to.*

"What did the doc say?"

"No doc; just the nurse, Gina. She said to keep wearing the sling like I have been." *And don't do what I'm about to do, but there isn't time to heal. Dr. Elmir could pack up any day.*

"So, no infection. Good. Uh, take care. Was that old woman you told me about still there?"

"She's bad off. They transferred her to get 'proper care.'"

"Oh." Doug put his truck into gear. "What's the plan? You said last night, 'We're going on tour.' You want to go back to the pit?"

"We're going everywhere. In sequence. I feel like in seeing those places again, we'll sense something. Our feelings might tell us what we're overlooking."

"To prove what's real. I get you. So, you want to start at the factory?"

"They scrubbed it clean, and it's impossible to get into. Regardless, that's Dr. Elmir's sector. Ugh. You saw him. He's immutable. He won't deviate from his recipe. He'll keep speaking with the same people he has been. It doesn't matter. There's something wrong we can't put our fingers on, but you and I, we're going to suss it out. It's not restricted to Milton. It's spreading, which means everyone we know is at risk."

"What then?"

"No clue. One thing at a time. Our first stop was my first stop: drive us to the dentist's."

"Yes, dear." He paused. "Sorry. That was weird." Doug pulled onto the street.

"Everything's weird in Milton." Na tightened her backpack's zippers. "Thanks. You're doing a lot. I'm not even paying for gas."

"No problem. Radio?"

"Off, please. Let's clear our heads, renew our perspective." Na folded her legs onto the seat and leaned her head on the seat belt strap. "Reboot, no sidetracking," she yawned. *Quietude.* Doug's bouncy-seated truck trundled and rumbled. Na blankly rocked, fluttered, and drifted down the street, block to block, limb to limb, leaf to leaf.

Doug nudged her sometime later. "Na, we're here." He stopped on the shoulder in front of the dentist's property.

Na came to and for a second thought Doug had driven to the wrong place. The house's alluring shroud of mystery had evaporated. Na saw it now for what it was: the decayed former residence of a remorseful recluse. "It's so ugly. You pass it every day?"

"Yep."

"Its time ended long ago. It wants to be demolished."

Doug jingled his keys and pumped his fist. "Shall we head to the cabin?"

"Definitely." Na slid out of the truck. The parched field emitted heat absorbed from the late-morning sun. "It's a fire hazard."

"Yeah." Doug started through the matted field.

Na caught up. "How often do you come here?"

"Not much, just to chase trespassers. A shout or two sends them running. 'Get lost, hooligans! Private property!'"

"Have you explored it yourself?"

"I explore to learn tales, and I already know his. It's sad."

"All stories are sad," Na mused.

"What do you mean?"

"Never mind. Let's head in." Na stepped on the cabin's fallen door for the third time and peered inside. Her face flushed like she'd been running fielding drills on a mid-September afternoon. Her scalp itched like a skin-peeling sunburn. *Is it hot? It's not hot.* Sweat dribbled down her temples. *What is this? Not shock. I'm fine. No fever. What is this?* "Doug, am I blushing?"

"No . . . ?"

"One sec." She nabbed a bottle of water from her backpack and took a gulp, sloshing her cheeks before swallowing. The water somehow left her mouth drier. She rubbed the roof of her mouth with her sticky tongue and massaged her skull with a quivering hand. *Ugh.* "I have to go back."

"To where you fell?"

"To the truck." *Dumbass*, she almost vocalized. *What's wrong with me?*

"Want my arm, in case you trip?"

"NO." Na began walking back with Doug close behind. "Er, thanks for the offer."

A minute later, Na reached the truck, scrambled inside, and left the door open for air. "Rrrrrrr-rah!" She tousled her hair with both hands. "It was that night again! I was bleeding and frail, a beached sea slug frying on the sand."

Doug squinted at her sympathetically as he climbed into the driver's seat.

"I had this grand fantasy. We were going to retrace our steps, notice something we missed, a detail or connection, and know where to go next. What the hell was I thinking? I can't go in there. And if I did, what's left to find?"

"A magic-mirror portal to an alternate universe?"

"I'm stupid." Na took another drink of water. "Now what?"

"Lunch? My house is literally there, up the street."

"Yes," she burped. "Lunch." Na patted her stomach and shut the door. "I'll eat what I brought from the hotel."

"We should refill our water too."

Doug's dark-red, vintage, two-story house with ivory trim predated the accompanying garage, a modern structure large enough for two vehicles. The buildings stood amid an untilled field less wild than the dentist's. The field's sharp edges and even height implied to Na that it had been productive not long ago. She wondered what his family had grown but was reluctant to ask. A loss like his would take her longer than three years to come to terms with, assuming she could ever talk about it.

Doug parked outside the garage. "Welcome to my humble childhood abode."

Walking between the buildings to the house's side door, Na estimated the garage was a few decades old. Weather exposure had discolored its foundation and eaves. Doug put his energy into the store, Na figured.

Inside, the house smelled distinctly of meatloaf. "Cooking?"

Doug led her into the kitchen and withdrew earthenware plates from white cabinets. "Yesterday. It's the single life. Cook once, eat for days." He handed a plate to Na.

"Thanks. Clean kitchen." It had a checkered, lemon-yellow-and-white linoleum floor. A white tablecloth covered a plain circular table. Na settled into one of three old, creaky chairs. "Expecting guests, or are you a do-the-dishes-now type?"

"Ants suck." Doug hefted an oval dish from the fridge, put it on the counter, and served himself.

"How about pets? An Oberhasli to keep you warm at night?"

"Ha. No. I'd feel bad, locking them up all day. It's just me and the wind."

"And the occasional trespasser." Na unwrapped her chicken salad sandwich over the plate and took a bite.

Doug filled glasses with water, put them on the table, and sat down with Na. "What about you? You're in college. What's your major?"

"I'm leaning toward physical therapy, but I'm not in the program yet. I have to apply by the end of this year if I want to graduate on time."

"Physical therapy? I can see that. You're, uh, strong. You lifted me like"—he snapped his fingers—"one-handed."

"Credit softball. Our pitcher wrecked her shoulder and got sent to PT. The strength and stability exercises they taught fixed her up. The entire team does them now during warm-ups."

"That's cool," Doug dithered and chewed. "What kind of music do you like?"

"Mostly . . ." Na kinked her neck and winced. *Again?*

"Your arm! I should've carried your backpack."

A sizzling tingle plucked at her left humerus. "Ngh. No. It's different." Needles strummed her sinew like guitar strings. Sharper and more metallic than a cramp, the threads of pain running the length her triceps suggested a direction. "What's upstairs?"

"My room, a spare bedroom, bathroom, storage. Why?"

"Go." Na didn't have a rationalization to give.

"I didn't—"

"C'mon." Na hugged her immobilized arm tightly against herself and left the table. Doug rushed ahead to escort her upstairs. The carpeted staircase was narrow and unsettlingly steep. Its handrail squeaked when Na put weight on it. Once at the top, Doug peeked into each room from the sparse hallway, never leaving Na's sight.

He shook his head. "Nada."

"Ow. Outside."

"How?"

Na turned too quickly and stumbled going down the second

step. *Not agai*— She clutched the handrail. Its brackets withstood the force of her fall, and she regained her footing. She collected herself and dashed downstairs and through the door.

"Where to?"

"Other side," Na ordered. They jogged around the house. A black cat lay in the dirt, its spine bent upwards in a V position. A bluish tongue extended from its open mouth.

"Shit. It's Tigre. What killed him? I'll call the neighbors."

"Take me back."

"Yeah, I need to get to the store too. I'll drive you and take care of Tigre later. Let me cover him first." He hurried off and returned with a bag. "He liked to roam. He was a good cat. Do you think he fell off the roof?"

"I don't know." The pain vanished. *A cat?*

39

BACK ON HER crispy hotel bed, Na doodled in her official research assistant notebook. She sketched the outline of a round clay pot with a long stem growing out. The pencil in her hand made short strokes to outline slender, pointed leaves. A second stem appeared with triangular projections at its tip. *A bird of paradise.* One of the projections, the bottom, elongated and curved into a lower jaw. Spiky teeth sprouted. Oblong adjacent teardrop shapes formed a head with an underbite and a bulbous eye. Na blinked at the finalized doodle; it had no meaning.

Just before two o'clock, halfway through Friday, her stomach turned from the medications she'd taken with breakfast. Skipping them yesterday had exacerbated their side effects. So had Tigre's tongue. She sipped bottled milk from Stuffs and reclined diagonally on the bed without changing her clothes. The liquid in her stomach gurgled when she shifted her head off the pillow and her shoes off the blanket. The New Mill Hotel's dry air and crispy white sheets had become familiar, like a cabin at summer camp. Between their sterile detergent scent and the milk's coolness, her stomachache lessened. A nap's heavy tendrils pulled her to the brink of sleep.

A somnambulating butterfly, she bobbed through half-dreamt mixtures of existence and imagination, rising and sinking amid tense dreamscapes and reality. *A two-hour mattress essay. Did I study enough? I need a pen. Pens have feathers. None of mine have feathers. Pillows have feathers . . .* With compressed eyelids and clenched fingers, she rose to waking awareness—*Not real, no tests*—and sank again. *They're shutting down the classrooms. They can't catch me.*

They'll think I'm stealing casserole and won't believe a word I say. She rose aloft and sank, and rose aloft and hovered midair. Na snapped on an invisible tether less than two meters long, suspended above an imperfect reflection of herself. *Not a dream.* The sleeping Na was expressionless, limp, and free of anxiety.

A slice of the world rotated on an axis. Kitty-corner to the hotel, a quarter turn out of alignment, spread a virtually vacant, brothy expanse. It bore an atmosphere of menace that riled Na's intuition: *Get out!* Her eyes blurred like a camera alternating its focus on the foreground and background. She settled on a midpoint nearer the bed. The hotel walls and furnishings had an inexplicable, ethereal quality from her disembodied vantage point. Their beiges, browns, and greens had faded to thin, insubstantial pastels. Through and around them splayed the expanse. She had no method of deciphering 3D doubled into six dimensions: *Where is true forward?*

Despite her confusion, Na recognized the connection and brought her hands together for assessment. They were as she pictured them, not as they were. She was slingless, and ink marks— an inevitable consequence of her brainless doodling—were absent from her thumbs. She had been here before, in the vaguest sense, and knew the expanse was inhabited. Dots and lumps wiggled uncertain distances away; the void had no background for scale. They were possibly figures, the exact figures she had encountered previously. *Krasue.* But nothing was clear. The expanse was as ethereal as her accommodations. *If the room is real, is everything real?* The prospect detonated a plasmic starburst: *Is this how I die?*

Once more stranded and vulnerable, Na flailed her limbs wildly in an attempt to swim back. Lacking resistance, water to stroke through, she didn't budge. She searched for the tether she felt and patted every centimeter of herself twice. There was no string with which to reel herself in. She was another wiggling lump confined to limbo.

A figure larger than the woods dweller approached. It possessed a presence full of heavy, melancholy radiance that transfixed Na's gaze. Naked, or at least unadorned, the masculine bulk was the color of a poorly lit closet hiding a venomous spider. Its deathly darkness was somehow more uniform than those others, but no less revolting. As it effortlessly coasted on a straight line, it seemed powerful and impossible to repel. *I'm not here. Don't see me. I'm not here.* Its trajectory was carrying it close, and the wake created by its movement churned the mist condensing at the fringe of Na's vicinity. It turned its head to Na and crumpled its face in sympathy. The figure was familiar. Too fast for Na to speak, its stable velocity swept it off into the fog.

It was harder to see now; the hotel and all its contents had thinned as the world cranked a half-turn awry. East, up, sideways, corkscrew were divided by zero and indiscernible. Time decomposed. Yet Na's unconscious vessel was distinct. *Return.* Na flailed in vain. *Return.*

A new figure emerged: pulsating, dim gray, feminine, brown-coated Krasue. It cackled soundlessly and slithered to the feet of Na's inert body. Tentatively, it prodded Na's left ankle. It poked Na's knee and ran a finger along her shin. At this, Na's ankle twitched. Apparently satisfied and unbothered by the hovering Na, it hunched down and brushed the outside of Na's right calf with its bubbling, tarry claw. It savored the interaction and nonverbally signaled, "Yumm."

Na blistered and peeled with hatred. *My bat. My bat will beat your wretched brains out.* Na imagined wielding her softball slugger: composite, brightly colored, branded with scratches on the E, and meticulously applied grip tape. She willed it to materialize by adding it to her self-image. *Mine. My hair. My nails. My bat. Essential extensions of me.* The bat refused to oblige.

Can't summon. I won't give up. On the rim of the white bathroom sink lay Na's bladed razor. Solid brick separated her from it, but there could be a line of sight through the expanse. The mist was the problem. She might be looking at it now, for all she knew. She needed a strong goal, a pinpoint motivator to bring it into view. That was why her body stayed clear, right? The razor must become a primal necessity, as it already was. *Krasue. I'll skin you like a serpent. Peel you like a kidney.* The white, plastic razor heard and answered. The fog evaporated. It shone under/beside/above her, just near enough to snag with an open umbrella. *Good. Come. Come slit.* But like the bat, the razor defied her summons.

I'll go to you. Damn teth— Ah-ha, I'm shackled! She grew heated at taking this long to understand. *Sever the cord. Snip for freedom.* Logically, her body's end of the tether had to be thicker, like a stream of dripping honey. Na pivoted, swinging her legs down toward her body. Groping with outstretched toes, she kicked at the air, praying she could break the tether. *Please . . . must . . . nngh.*

Krasue the puppeteer wholly ignored her. It was enraptured with eliciting spasms by poking Na's shell. A glutton at a buffet, Krasue waggled its digits between prods. It slunk from the base to the head of the bed and gleefully proceeded to explore Na's spine, whose twitches became jerks and jolts.

Krasue's salivating aura compelled Na to kick more fiercely, but the elusive tether was imperceptible. A frantic swoop of her leg sailed within a hairbreadth of her seizing vessel. At the instant of their proximity, Krasue howled, and Na's point of view deconstructed into the jumbled ruins of a defective stereogram. Her vision splintered into four, then reassembled into two, then one. She was back inside herself on the bed. The sloppy, grotesque Krasue had vanished, and the room was quiet.

Na's violent impulses swiftly waned, replaced with desperation. She lucidly chided herself, *What was I doing? Cutting the tether would've broken the link between me and my body. I'd have been cast off into the fog. It would've been suicide.* She deserved more self-recrimination than her energy permitted. Exhausted and bewildered, unable to tackle the threat Krasue posed, Na wrenched her cramping body off the bed and called Dr. Elmir on her phone.

"Yes, Na?"

"Wade died."

PART 4

ROJANA

40

ISOLATED WOMAN. OPEN. Calling us from cloth hut. No *cotèl*. A chance. A new way. Cleaner. Less stain.

Bizarre, she is. Amiss. Afloat. Spellbound. Supplicant. Asks for us. Any of us. She knows not. Others are damned. Aimless. Mad. Not I. I intend. I choose. They cower and admit. Admit sin. I keep them at bay. She is mine. A chance. A new way. Her prayer, my summons. My summons. I go between.

Vile stink. She is candles and grime. Clothed to bathe. Unsanctified life. Flies and soil. Endure her. Endurance is righteous. *Pecador.*

Hands on knees, she sits. Mouth open, eyes shut behind dark spectacles. Guilt. Hut cloth stifles sun. Does she see? Immaterial. Seeing or not, she feels. She will know I. With my thumb in her hand, she flicks. She feels and speaks. Is pleased? *Pecador.*

My thumb in her hand, her hand is my thumb. I intend. I control. Only her hand, thinner force, less fight. Cleaner. But useless. Only flicks. Need her wing. The stench. Give me strength.

Shoulder and shoulder. Abreast, I envelop her wing. Yes. Sears less than bowels. She speaks again, unlooking. Fool. She fights. I will not fail. Not Providence, am I. Her prayer. Do not fight me!

Resistance. She fights. Hammers, beats against herself. She cannot repel. I am fortress. Purpose. Supplicant, she will lose. Pointed, cat-eyed spectacles. Demonic. Shameless pecador. I focus and command. Take them. They are hers. They are yours. Remove with your wing that is mine. She fights. Jagged hot crackles.

She sees, at last. Screams at my purity. Gasps. Shrinks like a sinner. In knowing I, she regrets. She prayed and dares to hate. Bold pecador. Your sowing. Your reaping. By my hand you will spill and cease. My hand is your hand. Your spectacles are mine.

Her limb is my limb. She loses. Is defeated. I conduct and instruct. Hand clench, lift spectacles and sink. Sink into her. She is softness. All soft. I was soft and lost. Now, she too. Neck is softest. Spectacles are my knife. Drain your neck, pecador. Beat and spill. She sees, understands judgment. Knows her sins. Refuses acceptance. Fights more with her opposing hand.

Intruder. New hand, longer. Incompatible. A mismatched violator in our hut. Attached to woman, I cannot flee. New hand touches her. The searing! Unbelievable searing! I am blasted and repelled. Communion broken, I am cast out from between.

But I win. I am lossless. She knows and remembers me. She is changed by my hand.

I am changed. A new way. A cotèl. A chance. Renewal.

41

WHETHER IT WAS Chief Rawls's matter-of-fact personality or because Taryn had vouched for them, he asked forthright and unaccusatory questions.

Dr. Elmir and Na had hurried over when Wade didn't answer his phone. No, Dr. Elmir didn't consider Wade a risk for self-harm but had counseled Wade since losing his job and social circle. Wade's silver truck had been parked outside the wide-open garage, and they could see lights on inside his house. They tried knocking on the door and windows. Hearing nothing, they opened the unlocked front door and rushed inside.

"We left our shoes on. That would have bothered Wade," Dr. Elmir regretfully noted. Wade had been lying on his stomach on the kitchen floor. His neck and face were frigid. Dr. Elmir then called the police and Taryn.

Standing in Wade's driveway as they described these circumstances, Na thought about Wade's house. Yesterday it was a home. What was it now? How long for it to become an untouchable urchin? Decades ahead, would high school students tell stories and dare each other to enter? She wouldn't be in Milton to know. Well, she might return here, years in the future. The ebbing of time, its one-way current of more to less, reminded her of Wade's fate.

In movies, people were shaken by death. From centuries-old skeletons to recently deceased friends, lifeless bodies were jump scares. The main cast shouted and puked with the audience. Even hardened, stoic characters gasped at corpses. But Na knew beforehand, had watched Wade pass by. She didn't jump when they found him there in his kitchen. *Have I been desensitized?*

The loss of Wade, who had been unfairly blamed, was dreadful and premature and sad. Was he okay right now? What did death mean for Wade? The others she had seen, Krasue and its lot, were not okay. They were assailants, not victims—the opposite of fine. Would Wade devolve too?

Na had told Dr. Elmir everything on the way here. Despite his skepticism, he had answered her "hypotheticals." She had asked him why she couldn't swim and why she couldn't summon objects, when Krasue could do both. His best guess about moving was the tether, as she'd thought. The coat, Dr. Elmir confidently surmised, was an appearance attachment, a significant part of that person's self-concept, not an article of clothing that could be removed.

"Objects can't go from here to there," he'd said. The concept of soul attachments explained why ghostly possessions always corresponded with things the person had owned. It was also why their belongings deteriorated with the souls' sanity, breaking down and corroding as their owners' cruelty increased.

A small group of police now examined the scene. One officer barricaded and patrolled the driveway. Another officer called to Chief Rawls from Wade's garage. Chief Rawls tipped his hat and sauntered over while typing on his phone. Na, Taryn, and Dr. Elmir watched him as if waiting for a revelatory clue.

"How are you holding up, Taryn?" Of the three, Dr. Elmir had been the closest to Wade but showed no outward grief. He had retreated behind a veil of professionalism, and now, Na thought, tried to sustain it by counseling Taryn.

"The unelected de-facto mayor is surviving as best she can. There's a lot on a lot of plates, from economic consequences of rumors to the suspicions we inherited. Dr. Elmir—sorry, Zeb—said Jackson Mender is 'essentially harmless.' Those were your words, Na?"

"Spiritually harmless, in my opinion. My hunch is he's less meta- and more physical. He's no mystic."

"Sorry, come again?"

Shit. She doesn't know what I'm talking about. "Long day. I meant, he didn't target Mayor Handsom. I think he only cares about the herd in his pasture."

"Wade didn't know Jackson Mender, did he? I don't suppose Wade came up when you were undercover."

Na shook her head. Dr. Elmir answered, "Not as far as we know. He didn't attend their services, at least."

Rawls emerged from the garage and addressed them. "You're welcome to go home. An ME will have to tell us the cause. No note, no signs of OD. In the middle of cleaning, seems like. It was neighborly of you to come. Another guy lived alone too. He wasn't so lucky. Died in bed. It was a few days before the postman called us for a wellness check. Still waiting on his results. Same as here, though, foul play's unlikely. Just younger than you want to see. Well, that's two. Things come in threes, you know."

42

"**I SHOULD TAKE** you to the clinic. Prescient or not, you're unwell."

"It was a blip. A one-time thing."

"Two times." No amount of airing out had alleviated the business center's stuffiness. Nonetheless, Zeb found himself having a critical, uncontentious debate with Na.

"The first didn't count. I'm fine. Yes, except for my arm. We're getting somewhere. *Finally*. Don't start being overprotective now."

"Then I need earnest answers. I have to trust you're answering faithfully."

"I will," Na swore. "Shoot."

"Are you the tiniest bit dizzy? Can you keep your balance when you stand from a sitting position, walk, and go up stairs? Do you have double vision, see floaters or artifacts, or have eyesight distortions? Have you had headaches, felt uneasy or on edge, or had auditory hallucinations such as taps, clicks, or whispers?"

"No. Yes. Triple no. Triple no."

"Close your eyes. Listen inward. Could you will yourself to separate again? Is there a longing, a desire to return which tempts you to harm yourself?"

"Big no to harm. Hmm. I'm solid. I'm not picking anything up from . . . out there."

I have to take her word for it, but her voice has conviction. "You'll say if you get the smallest inkling that something's wrong? No matter if it's related to separating?"

"I promise."

"Fine. I'll say this: Your description fits. Like falling asleep or waking up, dying is a transition that muddles the mind as a person's grip on life slips. It's not a gate you hop through like that." Zeb snapped his fingers. "The tunnel cliché is an apt, common-sense representation. I believe you now, especially in light of Wade." *Conditionally believe. Perception is a process too. One sees Rubin's vase, another sees two faces.*

"Is this typical, this many ghosts and deaths?"

"Well, the other decedent, whoever that was, and Wade, rest his soul, we don't know either of their circumstances. Wade was . . ." *Just here. He was just here.*

"Except we do. Dr. Elmir, we know what led to this. Wade is fallout, departed thanks to whatever's happening here. He's not our fault—he's not *your* fault—and he didn't bring this on himself. He was silenced because he survived."

"Mm." *Wade was healing, not healed. Will he return? No. He was sad, not hateful. And Na said he passed on through the tunnel, as it were. But I can't be certain.*

"You've been at this for decades," Na interrupted. "How many ghosts have you seen yourself?"

"One."

"And?"

"I was eleven, doing what I always did at the beach. I dug a hole and tried to sculpt piles that replicated blueprints I'd drawn in my head. The rest of my family waded and snacked. Frolicked. I constructed a fort and trench. That day, the trench was shallow, two feet deep."

"Shallow?"

"Shallow for me. The sand was cold, and my fingers got numb. I figured it had rained that morning. As I dug and built, the sun moved and cast a shadow into my trench. You can't see ghosts in bright light; it washes out their luminescence. He was there underground, lying flat on his back inside my chilly trench, completely unfazed by my plastic shovel's scooping. I had introverted tendencies and didn't call anyone over. I just watched him and kept building."

"Did he have gross black holes? Clothing?"

"I remember he was old and had fancy clothes. Twenty is old to a kid, so I can't guess if he was thirty or seventy. I can't describe his fancy clothes either. It was too long ago. Memory is too unstable to describe him with confidence. But he wasn't threatening. He was a statue that didn't mind me or my digging. A wave eventually rolled up into my trench. He ignored that too. But the water eroded the trench and washed sand down, revealing a flask."

"Like a beaker?"

"A silver drinking flask, next to the spirit, nestled into the side of my pit. I didn't dare to touch it. Looking at him with a child's eyes, I believed he was happy and content because he had his cherished flask. I dug a narrow, deeper hole straight down, nudged the flask in with my shovel, and reburied it. I didn't want the lapping waves to reveal his treasure. I remember worrying, 'What if a beachcomber stole it?' I thought in those terms, that taking the flask would be stealing. The afternoon tide slowly brought more waves. My trench refilled with seawater and loose sand, and that's where my story ends.

"Today's me," Zeb continued, "an experienced adult, knows better. The spirit's sentimental fixation mutated him into a miserable shell. No consciousness, no personality. Had he been able to talk, he might have claimed happiness, but such madness is misery. Any warm emotions he got from his inanimate flask were figments. Flasks don't love. But that's where he wanted to be, underground, surrounded by damp, salty sand."

"Depressing."

"The only haunting he did was figurative; he was unforgettable."

"Can statues like him turn into vengeful spirits if their prized possessions are stolen?"

"For all the tales about spirits driven by revenge, evidence is lacking. Ghosts are—well, it's not a technical term—broken. Unthinking and irrational. A few have seemed conscious, but then again, pinpointing a living person's motives is tricky. It's the problem of other minds: how well can anyone know another's inner thoughts, etc."

"It's hardly academic when they're chasing you through the woods."

"Dogs chase cars. That doesn't mean they want revenge."

Na grabbed her backpack. "It's late. Good night."

"Good night, Na." *It is late, but not that late. Should I call Taryn, get the latest news?*

43

WHOOPS FROM IRRESPONSIBLE kids polluted Doug's night. He had delivered Tigre to his neighbors less than seven hours ago: "I don't know how, but it wasn't a car. He was in the grass behind my house. I'll miss him." Doug had left the neighbors to grieve and sought his own peace in the form of tea, meatloaf, and cheese crackers. But it was a clear night on a weekend's eve, and adolescents wanted thrills.

His family's rifle was locked in an upstairs cabinet. Angry brandishing would chase them off permanently, but that's how accidents happened. Instead, Doug donned a wide-brimmed hat and, on the way out, clicked his handheld, 5,000-lumens spotlight on and off. *Why do I care what these idiots do?*

Doug had a routine. He crossed the street and stealthily cut through the ruined house's front yard to catch delinquents unaware. Unlike strangers to the area, there was no chance of him stepping where he shouldn't. Midway through the intervening field, he aimed the spotlight at the cabin, switched it on, and screamed in a low, guttural voice, "Hey! Get lost!"

Most nights, that alone sent them scampering.

Tonight, a snide taunt echoed from behind the cabin: "Hey *what?* Get *what?*" An exaggerated "shhh" and laughter trailed.

Doug couldn't guess how many were here; none were in his spotlight's beam. It didn't matter. It was fine with him if their lives weren't already painful enough. "You want hurt?" Doug kicked his toe into the dirt and dug up an egg-sized rock. "Here's hurt!" He took a step, shifted his weight forward, and hurled the rock into a cabin window. The aged, single-paned glass split into large triangles that crashed into smaller shards on the cabin's floor. The rock, amplified by night's stillness, smacked an interior wall with a thunderous pop.

"Shit!" Twigs cracked and footsteps thumped as they retreated into the forest. These kids almost never parked where they could be easily caught and identified. Sneaking onto the property built tension and made their adventure more criminal, an added bonus. But some kids, snots especially, returned when the coast was clear. Less often, one hid just inside the cabin.

Quick sweeps of the retina-scorching light showed the entryway was free of stragglers. Next, he looked for anything that had been intentionally or unintentionally left behind. Kids almost never went into the chair room. They lingered outside and maybe poked into the first room, but the large inner room was such a deathtrap that almost no one entered, as far as he knew.

Except Na. She had come alone to investigate, not for mischief and cheap thrills. She had gone where no one went and ended passing out by the road.

Na's video hadn't captured everything. He tried to guess what she had thought and said as she explored. She would have noticed the dingy implements, but they wouldn't have stopped her. She'd have been locked on to the lumberjack's chair.

He hadn't meant to, but he began searching with the spotlight for signs of her presence. Dust, metal, wood, dirt, and handfuls of brown leaves blanketed the floor. Not far into the chair room, his light found three round spots on the floor. *Blood. Na's blood.* He knew, rationally, they could be anything. *That's crud, not blood. She could have fallen anywhere. But it is her blood. I sent her here.* Doug immediately turned and left.

He stood outside the cabin less than five minutes later, out of breath. A long hose with a nozzle lay at his feet. Long ago, it had watered his parents' crops. Doug's left hand held his lawnmower's gas can, which he had emptied onto the wall separating the cabin's rooms. A substantial gasoline trail led around and out, terminating on the busted door. *Go to hell.* He dropped the can, withdrew matches from his pocket, and set the door on fire. With a *fwump*, a blaze flashed inside and leapt up through the cabin's roof.

"He's crazy!"

I knew those snots were just hiding. Doug turned on the hose and soaked the weeds and brush around the cabin. It wouldn't be horrible if the house burned too, but the forest burning would hurt everybody in Milton. He knew his actions meant he couldn't sleep tonight, that he'd have to watch the wart roast into a lumpy pile of ash. It didn't matter. The dentist, Doug empathized, wouldn't have wanted to preserve a monument to his mistake.

44

SATURDAY

"HEY, NA. THANKS for coming with me."

"It was last minute, but I've dragged you everywhere." Na yawned. "And it's sunny and I'm hungry for breakfast."

Doug read his phone. "It's after ten. They're serving lunch."

"I slept in."

Doug traced a ring under his eyes. "I couldn't sleep at all, literally."

"So we average to normal. What's up?"

"Wait till the diner. Let's cut through the park; it's not crowded."

"Understatement."

Two romping retrievers played with their owners, whom Doug didn't know. The dogs wildly chased the Frisbee their parents zipped back and forth. With no topics springing to mind, Doug made idle conversation. "The diner's a block past City Hall."

"It's a huge park."

"Big enough for two soccer matches. Sports leagues practice year-round, even T-ball. There's no diamond, but grass is soft and more fun to slide on. I remember desperately wanting to show off for my parents, and whacking more of the tee than the ball. Thunk, flop, out. School teams have fields on the school grounds, but those are closed to the public because of vandalism and wire thieves."

"People love this park," Na softly observed.

"It's a hangout. Pretty much everywhere else is rugged forest or pastures. Don't picnic in a pasture."

Na stared at her feet. "You know Boone Hales at the museum?"

"He got me through state history. It was like Ms. Stumpfknell had moral objections to my graduation."

"Boone spoke bittersweetly about memories being linked to locations. There's no avoiding memories in small towns. Boone loves this park because it reminds him of his wife."

"Yeah?" Doug listened.

"It's a gravestone to me. A turfed epitaph. I met the mayor here. And Wade, in person."

"Wade? What happened?" An idea flashed into Doug's head: the lumberjack, angered by the cabin's destruction, had murdered Na's friend. He summarily discarded it. *More self-blame. This is about Wade and Na, not me.*

"They don't know. He died last night. Most people think his negligence killed his friends. I bet they label it suicide."

"Based on what I read . . ."

Na smashed a shoe into the ground. "Exactly why it's unfair."

Flirting was ludicrous. But Doug's attraction was an organic diversion in unnatural circumstances. Their nascent will-they-won't-they relationship drama protected him. Sickening horrors and life's gloomy destination were pit traps. Na, even at this moment, was his safety harness.

But they had shared days, not experiences. The park represented an accumulation of history to him. Footprints layered on footprints, each unique set related through blood and citizenship. If people made a town, new generations founded new towns on old stones. Na, understandably, felt none of that. Regardless of their differences, he vowed to back her up and give her his faith.

Doug motioned at a red-and-white-striped signboard ahead: "Birch Knot, the best when nothing's open. Its popularity is a mystery."

"Isn't that Dr. Elmir's car?"

"Weren't you with him a few minutes ago?" Doug glanced backward, as if the hotel's vehicles were still visible.

"I haven't seen him. And he didn't leave a message. He's going easy on me," Na flatly reported.

"Yeah, good." *Double good: change subjects. Nothing can be done about Wade.* "How are you?"

"Eh."

"Bad day?"

"Eh. I'm fine. Strange he's here. We're sitting separate. Since he doesn't want me busy, we're not having a working breakfast."

"Suits me." Doug had invited her here in the first place to get public privacy.

Through the central front door, a front desk divided the restaurant's bright red-and-white interior into halves. The desk was unmanned, but a server hauling armfuls of dirty dishes promptly greeted them. "He-ey," she drawled. "Have a seat. We'll be right there."

Doug hesitated, and Na whispered, "Back booth." She had noticed them before Doug: Taryn and Dr. Elmir, chatting over mostly empty plates which had been pushed aside.

"We'll keep it brief," Doug confirmed.

The restaurant had few customers. Three families were seated in the right half, one of which displayed a birthday banner. A sprinkling of pairs and singles occupied the left half. Upon reaching Taryn's table, Na led. "Morning, Dr. Elmir."

"Na, Doug, I'm apologizing to Taryn for sending her down a multitude of dead-ends. Her father was right: heartbreaking losses aplenty, but no prior history of what we've seen—you've seen. What are you two up to?"

He. Is. Sapped. Doug spotted bereavement's toll in Dr. Elmir's dulled poise and hollow eyes propped up by squinting. Doug had sunk into the same mood the year after his parents' death.

"Brunch," uttered Na.

Dr. Elmir tapped a dish. "Milky eggs, if that's your taste."

"I'll mosey through the menu, see what's good for my stomach. Why hurry, right?"

"Yes. No hurry today, Na, and we're not heading home yet. But this is too grim for a sophomore novice. I shouldn't have teetered back and forth about your role. You believe you're fine now. Great. Fine. But trauma sneaks up and leaps out once your mind's done processing. Or worse, it manifests years later as your perspective changes, when your kids are sophomores in college.

"Succinctly, you've been definitively damaged physically, and possibly psychologically. Relax. Heal. I trust Doug to watch over you. But keep your energy up. I'll ask when I need help with fitting tasks. To wit, it's a slow week in the office for you, not a furlough."

"Fine by me. We're going to order. I haven't eaten. Take care, Taryn."

"You two too." Taryn smiled back.

Doug waved and trailed Na. He asked again, "You're really okay?"

"Legitimately."

In their own booth far from their elders, Doug handed Na a wrinkled laminated menu he'd nabbed from a neighboring table. "No recommendations. Go with your gut."

"What's spiral-cut chicken?"

"Jokes: their shtick."

The server neared their table. "Are y'all ready?"

Na passed the menu to her. "Regular grilled cheese and water."

"Cobble-cobble salad for me."

Cringe. The server nodded and departed.

"And water, please," Doug called after her.

Na grimaced. "You have something to tell me? Don't delay on my account."

"More trespassers messed around in that cabin last night, the dentist's. I . . . lost it. I took a gas can and burned it to cinders." Doug switched gears before delivering the punchline. "That's why I couldn't sleep. Now you can't go back. It's gone, and so's the lumberjack."

Na gaped. "Wish you'd done it a month ago. That eyesore was the only Milton address *not* haunted."

Doug swept away his questions about her desire to meet the

lumberjack. Na was irritated and wanted peace, it seemed. Being there for her, supporting her, didn't mean needling her into talking. Her mood was familiar to Doug. When he was mired in dejection, quiet was all he wanted too. Their meals arrived quickly, and they ate in anxious silence.

Na aligned her utensils on the rim of her plate. "I'm heading back."

"Me too."

"I don't need an escort."

I'm supposed to watch over her. She's upset, though. "I have to open Stuffs," Doug defended, "but you go. I'll stay and pay."

Doug jogged back through the park not five minutes later, trying to drain excess energy from his overcharged battery. In that short time alone, he tallied a shamefully long list of mistakes he'd made during the hour spent with Na. *I'm exhausted*, he consoled himself. *And everything considered, her moodiness is justified.* His full gut gurgled from sleep deprivation too. A sonorous, bubbly warble preceded a loud burp. But it was a weekend, and Doug couldn't excuse another day away from Stuffs. He switched to high-knee jogging to aid digestion.

At the far side of the park, his hopping turned to sprinting. Ahead of him lay Na, motionless and face down in the grass, mere inches from the sidewalk. Her hair splayed about her. He thought better of flipping her over, in case she'd hit her head. *Oh God. How far's the truck? One, two blocks?* He dialed 911 on his own phone and puked.

45

"**CONFIRMED SHE'S STABLE,** Kath. Vital signs good. The sling means meds—might explain her unconsciousness."

"Alright, Martin. I'll radio the clinic. Odds are she's one of theirs." Milton's old center had square corners and a tidy layout. Outside town, the roads were wandering squiggles. In their wisdom, Milton's forefathers had opted to pave disjointed logging routes trampled by 1800s laborers. "Sharp turns ahead, so—"

"The usual, got it. Say, Kath, can you turn down the A/C?"

Mid-reach for the radio, she diverted her hands to the ambulance's dashboard knobs. Vent: check. Fan: check. "It *is* down. It's *off* off."

"Couldja triple-check? It's freezing back here."

"Really?" Martin never teased when they had a patient on board. Kath glanced up at the mirrors. Before her eyes, Martin's face coagulated into mortuary wax. In more than a decade as an EMT, she had not seen a man this shade of ochre. His arm stiffened into a club and slammed the side of her head. She would bruise, but Kath was more worried about her partner. "Martin!"

A crash would be worse. She looked back at the road and tucked inside her seat, bracing for more hits as she tried to maintain control of the ambulance. The hits kept coming, one after another. Some thumped harmlessly against the front passenger seat, as if he couldn't aim his strikes. "Martin!"

The next hit her ear, rippling heat through her skull and knocking her glasses crooked. The distortion from her lenses made it hard to steer cleanly. Her trained arms automatically adjusted to the new visual input and oversteered. Kath braked and closed an eye to minimize the distortion and correct their course.

Too late. Martin's next swing jammed forward into the wheel. The ambulance veered into the rocky embankment and rolled onto its side. The impact threw Martin toward Kath. Dazed and concussed, she tried running through emergency procedures: *Howzit patience, howzit patience.* Nothing made sense. Goose bumps rose along her arms. She felt cold.

Kath heard a rumble, an engine, and . . . whines? Suddenly, she felt heat again in her face and legs. Waxy Martin stretched into a vista of agony and regret, then wheezed and crumpled onto the van's bottom side. "Mar—" Kat didn't finish his name before she blacked out, just like their securely fastened passenger.

46

IRRITATION BROUGHT NA back: she railed against the iciness running up her forearms. "Cold!" The metal buckles on her restraints held fast.

"Hello, Ms. Bensen," a man's muffled voice rippled. He must have been wearing a mask or lurking behind a partition. Captured like Na was, it relieved her that he was not at her bedside.

"Where am I? I can't move. I can't see. Why am I blindfolded?"

"Do you remember what happened?"

I remember being ticked. "I was in the park." *Shit, I fainted. How did I . . . ?*

"You had a seizure."

"I haven't shaken, like, ever."

"The blindfold is protection. Visual stimuli exacerbate seizures. Some devices—the cardiogram—have aggravating lights. A single seizure could cause catastrophic damage."

"Why am I tied up?"

"More protection. Healthy patients without preexisting conditions hurt themselves during tremors. They fall or twitch and gore themselves on objects. For you, belts and cuffs are doubly important." The man's mechanical voice disquieted Na; its professionally removed tenor lacked Gina's solemn tinge. Yet his voice had intensity. "Your stupor has broken. But it may recur. You are as safe as I can make you. This is temporary, I assure you. After all, you must be mobile to evaluate the treatment. When I am confident you have stabilized, treatment will resume."

"What should I do?" *What can I do?*

"You are a curiosity. Plausibly unique. Listen to me. Together we will unearth the roots of your crisis."

"How about when I need to get up?"

"Your disorder is severe. Meditate. Sleep. Do not despair: you are being carefully watched."

"So, what, holler? Hello? Are you there?" *W-T-F does that mean?*

She had forgotten to ask his name. *And where the hell am I? Is it weird that I'm still in my clothes?* The man had her records, which seemed like a good sign. If she wasn't in the clinic, she was somewhere in their network. *I'll know for sure if Gina comes. She'll come if this is the clinic.*

Sedation was the only explanation Na had for sleeping again. Instinctively, she swung her legs sideways off the bed to get up and use the bathroom. As she sat up, she returned to the here and now by replaying her most recent memories. *Am I late for a class or appointment? Do I need a shower? How does my arm feel? Where did I slee— Blindfolded, tied to a bed.* But she opened her eyes nonetheless, and saw herself.

Separate again, tethered and weightless, a bubble in her core inflated with despair. She had barely repossessed her body last time. She had lost her cool and begun to degrade. But she'd survived, which provided a tiny thumbtack of determination to do better. *I will not be Krasue, lost and forever hungry.*

Na snagged an idea, a benefit, from the rim of her scrambled mind. *The blindfold doesn't matter.* Physical reality remained gauzy and askew. Competing overlays of existence flitted in and out of focus. A thin, invisible tether still confined her in this otherworldly vacuum, holding her near her body, and she could not explore beyond her vicinity. *Thank goodness.* Her room had long gray walls, dim lighting, square meters of empty space, and an underground, basement-like coldness. A curtain was drawn around a second bed on the opposite side of the spacious room. This was not the clinic. It was a cell. *This feels all wrong.*

A shell rolled in on a wheelchair pushed by a man. Na knew the slumped, lifeless husk was alive, but not how she knew; it contained energy. The man, in contrast, had double solidity. His body and spirit overlapped perfectly. They unified a point occupying two realms, and Na felt drawn almost like gravity. He ushered the wheelchair to the curtained bed and spun it so the shell faced the door. He ignored Na completely and exited without a word of comfort for either patient. *Is he the doctor from before?* She had to move quickly.

Krasue. Krasue's prodding had made Na's body twitch and spasm, which meant Na could too. And Na had more freedom now, a lightness different from the massless suspension she'd experienced before. The tether was pliable and lax. With a thought, Na gracefully slid downward next to the bed. The optical confusion from being locked askew and out of sync could be managed because Na knew what to search for. A corded nurse call ran along the bed and ended next to her physical hand. She had to press the button on that clicker.

Na touched her actual hand with her spirit's. As before, a swirling screech of visual noise threatened to suck her back into her drugged, immobile body. *Not yet.* She held back, pushed herself away, and clawed at the appendage with pumping grips. *Come on. Come on.* Her hand flinched at first, a tiny flick of the wrist, then seized and crushed the call with force that turned her knuckles white. Victorious and unable to resist the pull longer, Na succumbed and dispersed back into her incapacitated self.

47

ZEB HUNG UP. He'd been right about Na needing observation and was grateful for Doug's assistance, despite the dilemmas caused by his involvement. Once more, Na had to be given precedence over his work. *Trouble looks for her as much as she looks for it.*

Doug said she hadn't responded to his texts or messages, so Zeb's first call was to the clinic. They knew Zeb was responsible for her and could tell him things they couldn't tell Doug. The receptionist agreed with what Doug had said, that an ambulance would have taken Na to their clinic, yet she was not there. Furthermore, no ambulances had radioed to say she was inbound. As far as they knew, Na was fine.

He called Taryn. "Hello, it's Zeb."

"Hey, Zeb! Thanks again for the meal."

"Sure, sure. Listen, I need your help. Na's missing."

"What?"

"Doug called 911 after she fainted in the park. They picked her up, and that's the last we've heard of her. She's not at the clinic, which is where everyone says she should be. I'm stumped."

"Hold on. An ambulance came and got her?"

"That's what Doug said, yes."

"There was a crash earlier. An ambulance lost control and went off the road. I had to send a crew to divert traffic. The paramedics lived. They're still getting treated, I think."

"What?! When I asked the clinic, they said they didn't have any patients like that. I asked just in case they had her and couldn't ID her. Did they lie to me?"

"Oh, no, the crash was on one of those looping roads that goes around the town, faster but longer. Where it was, they shuttled the victims to Veronica Hospice instead. I *think* that's why. I don't know. Anyway, they've got a small emergency ward. I bet that's where she is."

"Can you give me directions? I don't think they can tell me anything over the phone."

"Why don't you pick me up? I'm not doing anything my dad can't. And the route there isn't direct because that road is closed."

"Yes. Good idea. I'm heading there now."

48

A NURSE HAD answered her call just as the doctor had promised, which gave Na a tidbit of reassurance that she wasn't in immediate danger. After using the restroom, Na had been strapped back into bed. She asked to be left unrestrained, but the nurse had shrugged and reapplied the buckles and blindfold. Those ten minutes after he answered her call were a blur from the mixture of sedatives, sleep, and disorientation. The nurse might have been the same man who had brought in the wheelchair.

Stationary like this, Na found herself reaching out again. If she was going to keep separating, it seemed like a good idea to practice reunifying. What if she hadn't been on a hotel bed, or with Doug in the woods, or in a public park?

With minimal effort, Na rose vertically and alongside her hospital bed. The tethers were no stiffer than an hour ago, and terra firma no clearer. She acclimated by symbolically extending her incorporeal limbs and spreading her fingers and toes. *These are mine? They don't have muscles, do they?*

Behind the chair-bound shell across the room, a figure grew like a shadow on the wall. Unmistakably deliberate, the wheelchair crept toward Na, and the shadow grew. *Shit. Something. Someone?* The silhouette was not Krasue's. *I'm not weak. I'll fight this time.* Each inch closer made another detail discernable: a cloth-draped figure bearing a cruel countenance distinctly more human than Krasue's. *It couldn't be.* The cloth was printed with the cross of Toulouse. *Another soldier from their army? Are they at war with Milton, with us, with . . . my family and me?*

Two words riddled with animosity inexplicably reverberated in Na's mind. *Pecador. Cotèl.*

This thing was entirely different from the skittish shapes and maliciously curious forms Na had already met. This thing had thoughts. Drives. It had wants and reasoned about how to achieve them. As fearsome as it was, it approached Na furtively.

Na could make out details of the shell, too. Hunched and slumped sideways, it exposed its scalp and the scruff of its neck. A row of staples and stitches familiar to Na marked the neck. A new, similar ring circled the crown of its skull. *Her* skull, the woman Na had saved at the clinic—no, a remnant of her. Na's first impression was correct. The woman who cried for chalk had abandoned her vessel. Or she had been evicted.

A pit of horrified loathing yawned inside Na. As a spirit, she had no guts to churn. Here in this room, she also was being made a shell. *This is not the clinic.*

The Toulouse spirit eyed Na quizzically. Na wondered what had attracted it here to begin with. Every time Na separated, specters appeared. *Do two unoccupied bodies in one place emit a stronger signal, attracting higher-level ghosts? Do ghosts have levels?* Whatever the case, it occurred to Na that it might not be seeing what she did. It had partially possessed the shell, possibly restricting its view to the physical. Outside of her body, Na saw aspects of both worlds. Attached to the shell, Toulouse crept and dragged the wheelchair nearer.

You want war? Fine. Today, I get first strike.

A hot glare burst from the ceiling and propelled Na back inside herself. Her wound burned with caustic pain. She cried out, "Haaaaaangh!"

The strange doctor's mechanical voice broadcast over a speaker: "One moment. I have a guest to meet."

49

ZEB'S TOLERANCE FOR Veronica Hospice's assistants had run dry. "You cannot deny you received the crash victims. I know they're here. Taryn"—he pointed—"knows they're here. We know you're lying. Tell us the truth, or we'll take this up with my colleagues on your licensing board." It was not an empty threat, and Zeb sternly said it as such.

One of the two assistants gently hung up his phone. "Dr. Nathyn, the manager, is on his way."

"Another lie?" Zeb made a fist.

"Dr. Elmir, I am Dr. Saul Nathyn. Pleasure to meet you." The man entered the office from behind the assistants and came to the desk. He had a starchy walk and spoke with a drumbeat rhythm that implied power and irreverence. He kept his thick, dark, lightly graying hair neat, and wore elegant glasses with thin lenses.

"Dr. Saul Nathyn? I know your name. Nathyn with a 'y'?"

"Yes."

"You're a pharmacist. Or *the* pharmacist of Milton, I should say." *All the pills Wade took bore his name, as did Na's.*

"Yes, I am one pharmacist, but not the only. In addition, I founded and manage this facility for the terminally ill. Having watched people needlessly suffer due to undermedication, I created a better place. Our residents are offered nepenthes without unwarranted fears of addiction and abuse."

"I understand your goal, but that's not why we are here. My own assistant, Rojana Bensen, is missing. Earlier today you admitted two EMTs who were in an ambulance accident. Your assistants here are unwilling to admit that fact. Rojana was in that ambulance as well."

"We're not just asking," Taryn interjected. "Rojana is part of an ongoing investigation that has the support of the mayor's office."

Dr. Nathyn maintained his businesslike demeanor. "The mayoral position is vacant now, I understand. My condolences." He reached out to shake both of their hands. "The ICU is at the far end of the building. My assistants here primarily arrange meetings between our patients and their guests. They would not know that both were treated. Since then, one has been released to a guardian. The second was arrested shortly afterward for suspicion of assault."

"So, they're not here," Zeb challenged.

"They are not."

"And did you admit a third person today, a young woman who might not have had identification?"

"No. We only took in two EMTs," Dr. Nathyn steadfastly claimed.

His double-talk exasperated Taryn. "How can you be certain? Didn't you just say patients are treated here without your support staff's knowledge?"

"Honestly, you must believe it. Trust is your best option. Out of respect for the privacy of our residents, I cannot allow you to tour my facility in search of her. Regrettably, this conversation is as helpful as the law permits me to be."

Zeb covered their bases. "Where else do Milton's people receive medical care, besides this hospice and the Milton Medical Wellness Clinic?"

"None, assuming she is receiving care from a licensed provider." Dr. Nathyn paused and forebodingly added, "Perhaps you should involve the police?"

"Well, thank you, I guess. We'll discuss our options and leave you to your work." *Maybe Doug has suggestions. Na trusts him as a source, and he called the ambulance. He deserves an update.*

"Until next time, Dr. Elmir, Ms. Hales." Dr. Nathyn nodded.

50

"HOW DID YOU get over here?" An ounce of certifiable astonishment leaked into the man's dispassionate tone. Na heard the wheelchair creak away. "Forgive the interruption," he resumed, "and the lights, if they disturbed you. Rojana, I met your mentor, Dr. Zebediah Elmir." An old chair's casters squeaked and rattled across the tile floor. "He is concerned for your safety. With that in mind, we will begin the next phase of your treatment."

Na clenched her teeth from the pain that had abated only slightly. *It's just pain. Think. Dr. Elmir came. Was I wrong? Is this the clinic?* But he hadn't visited, which meant they'd stopped him. *If he's sick like me, it's food poisoning. Listeria, salmonella, E. coli. Was it the restaurant or the hotel? I've been sick a while; it had to be the hotel. What's this 'next' phase of treatment? Were meds phase one? I've been sleeping a lot, I think. It's hard to tell. I need answers. Play nice.* "Am I done with the blindfold?"

"This next phase is critical. Absolutely critical. I cannot stress that enough. Needles will be involved, to administer drugs."

"I'm fine with needles."

"Very well. I shall remove the blinder."

For the first time, Na examined the room and its occupants from her physical body. Except for her shoes, she was in fact still wearing the clothes she'd put on that morning. The sling had been removed. Straps firmly held her arms and shoulders instead. The slumped woman in the wheelchair now faced the curtained bed more than six meters away.

Having stood to remove the blindfold, the man loomed over Na.

His face and style of eyewear duplicated his voice's abundance of confidence and dearth of geniality.

"I imagine you are unaware of Dr. Elmir's importance to his field." The man sat in his old chair and scooted over to a rolling storage cabinet. He began opening drawers and arranging small objects on the cabinet's top. "His body of work supplied mine with direction. I had been unsuccessful until adopting his perspective."

"I don't follow. Isn't his, um, specialty, looked down upon?" *Careful, you don't know what he knows.*

"Depending on who you ask. By the by"—he shifted to look at her squarely—"my name is Dr. Saul Nathyn. I have been observing and managing your case from the beginning. It is time you knew my name." He donned a surgical mask and resumed fussing with the cabinet's contents. "You see . . . Ah, where to begin. Individuals vary in every conceivable way. Intelligence. Handedness. Personality. Sexuality. Each individual's mind has a certain affinity for its host, its body. In most, such as mine, that affinity is quite high. Yours is low."

"Low?"

"You need scale. In percentages, it is approximately fifty percent, indicative of partial compatibility. Partial unity. I believe one cause of your low affinity is genetic. You and likely your relatives, perhaps your entire family, tend toward low affinity. Your children, if you had children, would have low affinity. One moment. I will come back to this, to you." Dr. Nathyn rotated his seat for several minutes and concentrated on items out of Na's view.

"My work today," he continued, "centers on that affinity. The creation of a person forms two components, a mind and a body. Not exactly two—I am simplifying. A brain and its nervous system are the conduit through which a mind owns a body. A brain is an antenna; a mind is a radio station. The precise structure of a brain determines which radio station can, or cannot, be received. Some brains are strongly attuned to their minds, some weakly. That is affinity. The conclusion, the obvious application of this theory, is to modify a brain, to change its channels, to decrease its affinity for its natural mind and increase its affinity with another. Understand?"

Shit. "You want to swap bodies. You want immortality."

"You *do* understand. Finally, an intelligent subject. Your intelligence will aid the next step. This combination I am preparing will eject your mind. At that moment, I ask you to inhabit the woman there." Dr. Nathyn indicated the wheelchair. "You must cooperate to live. An unhoused mind soon grows disoriented and deteriorates into phantom, detestable beings less valuable than insects. She has been customized and is ready to receive you. From my observations, I hypothesize that you will feel attracted to her, pulled. I have validated that broken or empty vessels attract the attention of homeless spirits. Once you are there, send a message, a signal of your choosing. I will reverse the effects, and you will be restored."

"Restored like this will heal me? It will stop my fainting and these out-of-body experiences?"

"No, Rojana. Nausea, dizziness, fainting are side effects of medications I have given you. Their remedy is plain: cease the treatment. Your experiences, however, are incurable."

"I'm sick because of you?"

"Ah, Rojana, you are fit and healthy. You have tolerated the medication considerably better than my other subjects. I find too many in less than ideal condition. Most recently, I lost a candidate who was debilitated when he fell under my care. Something to do with pneumonia. Losing him was unfortunate. Then, in restitution, serendipity or Providence brought you to me sooner than I had intended."

Wade. "Why?"

"Here, in this room, you have been outside yourself and seen me, yes?"

What's safe to tell him and what isn't? "Um, yes."

"You saw my body and mind, moving as one."

"Yes."

"You cannot apply that ability to yourself because you only have such sight when you are divided. If you could examine yourself . . ." He sighed. "Alas, there are no mirrors with such powers. Myths about magical mirrors are lies."

"So why—"

"It is another of your special properties. It is why you must do what I request and the second, most critical reason why your affinity is low. Your mind and body are not one. Your mind, your—I despise this word—soul is larger than your body. You do not fit inside yourself. Thus, you are not the original Rojana."

"What?" Na strained against her cuffs.

"Fascinating. You are surprised. You were unaware of the fact. Therefore, your possession of Rojana is accidental or completely forgotten. It is impossible to know which. As Dr. Elmir theorized, leaving your corpse and this world and then returning distorts and defiles the mind. However, you have proven quite sane. I wonder if that gives us hints about who you initially were. I wager that *if* your first body died, you were not dead long. But the end is the same. I cannot yet increase your affinity for your current body. That is an end goal of my research. Today you will remain as you are, not whole and only partially alive. Steady yourself."

"Wait, you ca—"

Saul injected a substance into Na's shoulder and flipped a switch on one of the blinking devices. Their combined effects powerfully expelled her, giving her reversed symptoms of snapping back to her body. Coherence split into six directions of intangible holograms that Na was just barely beginning to comprehend. A new lightness also permeated her; her tethers had weakened or, Na dreaded, been totally severed. She didn't dare to dwell on it.

I don't like this. He can go to hell. Na attempted to reenter herself and lay her hands on her physical waist. A static-like zap knocked her back. Had she been physical, she would have stumbled backward onto the floor. She had no choice. Saul forced her cooperation.

The vacant shell attracted her, and despite being able to resist, Na allowed it to guide her in. She drifted across the room, further from her body than she'd ever been, and considered what to do. The Toulouse ghost had demonstrated a method absolutely preferable to complete possession. Like him, then, she moved behind and over the woman's husk, partially encompassing her. In this position, Na detected threads of energy, thin stripes within the shell which marked life: neuronal electrical activity. Guessing they were interactable, Na moved herself along their pulsating flow, down the shell's torso, arms, and legs in a motion akin to dancing. Na's sequence carried the woman's shell forward.

The wheelchair drifted to Saul, and his lips grinned tightly in self-satisfaction. Partially within the old, brain-dead woman, Na heard him speak.

"Good, Rojana. That body belongs to you, a gift for your assistance. This arrangement is doubtlessly preferable to your death for us both. You live, and I may ask you questions which arise. I have need of this body, your old host. In addition to its favorable condition, it appears to have become unusually receptive, or perhaps sensitive is a better word, to the movements of spirits in its area. I believe the injury to your arm, the exposure and damage to its nerves, caused it. In any case, thank you for this specimen. Not that it was truly yours in the first place. Out of deference and gratitude, I shall not modify it in your presence."

51

MISTY DARKNESS ABSORBED Na. Clouded fury curled and peeled flakes from her disembodied soul's skin as she surrendered to vengeance. Bubbles began to percolate between her skin's slits. *I will make him bleed and pay. And bleed.*

A loud bang echoed in the cave-like room. "You were not invited to stay, Dr. Elmir. All of you are disrupting my lab."

Rescue? A hint of support, of hope, shoved Na in the right direction. With effort she had practiced a few times, she recollected herself and surveyed the room's entrance. Saul stood defiantly, a man accustomed to using status and self-confidence to ensure obedience. Doug, Taryn, and Dr. Elmir, who had barged through the door, were frozen in place, either from shock or Saul's boldness. She could only guess at what they saw inside the room: a bound, unconscious Na lying on a bed, an amoral man lusting for immortality, a disfigured elderly woman, and the ghost of Na herself hovering around the woman.

"Let Na go!" Dr. Elmir shouted.

"She is ready to leave. You may have her." Saul motioned at the elderly woman. "But let's avoid an unlawful confrontation. This belongs to me." He raised a scalpel and held it over Na's trachea. "I have wrested it from Rojana's control as she wrested it from its previous tenant."

"I don't understand," Dr. Elmir pleaded.

"You have fallen behind, Dr. Elmir. Go back to your university and meditate on what you can glean from Rojana. Then you may come to appreciate my advancements based on your theories."

Na wished to explain and warn them off, but her possession of the woman was incomplete. Doug, horrified, stared at her, not her body, from behind Dr. Elmir. He seemed unable to digest the scene, perhaps stuck in grief from losing someone else. Na recognized his uncertainty as he waited for something to happen. Taryn leaned toward the door and likely planned to run for help.

Suddenly, Na recalled how different Krasue looked in the two realms, and wondered how much of her own spirit was visible under the room's lights. Even a basic gesture like "back off" might be wasted on the three who came to rescue her.

Krasue gave Na inspiration. At the burn pit and in the hotel, the vile mass had been nearby when Na separated. Something in Na interested it. *Do we both have affinity to my body? Is it my body? No, stop, don't be gullible. This guy's a snake. He wants me confused and powerless.* With her spiritual mind, Na cried out, "Krasue! Hungry? Feed! Krasue! Hungry? Feed!" She repeated the phrase like a planetary beacon to the stars.

Krasue responded. It shimmered into view through the soupy ether, waggling its claws at the prospect of a disinhabited, defenseless Na. Ignoring all others, it went straight for Na and tested the body with its hand. Just like Na herself, Krasue's poke bounced off like it had tapped an electric fence.

If I can't get in, you can't either. Now . . . The shell's attractive force had snagged Na and could not be ignored, but it could not suck her in. Na's best guess was the woman was too ravaged to sustain life and could not trap her soul. Na relaxed, released her connections to the shell, and willed herself to slide over to Krasue. As Na left the woman in the wheelchair, she saw Doug look away and around the room. *They can't see me now. Okay.*

The distance was just a few meters, but the turbulent expanse had a gaping maw which sought to swallow her. Krasue's appearance had left a wake. Or perhaps this location, a hospice, had a current from the traffic of the newly deceased. Tetherless as she traveled, Na felt a new draw, a wink in the distance. *Focus. No time.* Willpower and desires were the fuel in this state, and despite its repugnance, Na needed to reach Krasue.

Krasue had attempted to consume Na. Because of that, Na understood it. Krasue seethed with envy—a more precise word than hunger. Saul was the same, a madman jealous of something no one had. Like the empty woman's, Saul's body contained energy. His energy had strength and intensity, vitality, and within it, Na beheld threads. *They deserve each other.*

Na reached her left hand out and plunged it inside Krasue, who was fixated on Na's healthy body. It howled unpleasantly with a mixture of ecstasy and rage. Inside, Na touched the frayed remains of tethers, strands that had once bound this rotted soul to humanity. With her right, Na deftly, gently plucked a strand from Saul. He twitched as if a muscle had twanged from an old strain but maintained his guard and kept his eyes on the other three.

Surprisingly easily, without effort or tension, Na drew her hands together and intertwined the separate threads. They spliced readily, a sign the two yearned to be greater. Krasue turned, stared directly into Na's spiritual face, and exorbitantly smiled. Na dropped the tether in disgust. It spun and retracted back into place within Saul. Saul now owned two souls.

The splice was unnatural, and Saul bore the brunt of the sin. Krasue interwove with him, devouring his vitality and fusing with his fibers. The two did not wholly merge; they remained apart within the same house. Saul's body jerked and shook from the conflict inside it, and he tossed himself onto the floor. The scalpel skittered away. Doug, Dr. Elmir, and Taryn waited for him to stop flailing, ready to pounce. But he did not stop swinging, so they stayed back by the entrance, away from Na.

52

NA COULD NOT repossess herself yet. Unable to speak through her own mouth or the old woman's shell, she waited and hoped for an opportunity to shut down Saul's devices. *They still can't see me?*

Saul's squirming preoccupied Dr. Elmir and Doug, leaving Taryn to approach the physical Na first. She began to undo the restraints. As soon as Taryn unbuckled Na's torso, Na dove elbow-deep into her uninjured shoulder. Taryn leapt backward. *Okay, she can now, maybe.*

The resistance Na felt earlier had subsided; she was not instantly rejected. That first dose of Saul's concoction had to have been small. Na struggled to make her physical self sit up. It was futile. In her detached state, the necessary movement was too great. Heaving her limp body to the device's switch amounted to deadlifting a soggy bale of hay. Mid-strain, the device clicked off. Na caught a glimpse of Taryn by the wall, holding a cord. Just as the power cut off, Na ragdolled back home to her body at last. Bleary from unconsciousness and mentally exhausted, she welcomed them with a cough. "Thanks."

"Are you all right?" called Dr. Elmir.

"Ungh." Na gingerly sat up, cradling her right elbow with her left hand. "Yes. No. My arm hurts because of him. It. Them."

Doug slid to the ground and panted. "I'm glad you're okay," he huffed. "I might be sick."

Dr. Elmir abandoned his station near the door and strode to Taryn's side. "What did you do to that bastard, exactly?"

"Could you tell? I kind of joined them, Saul and Krasue. He made me go there"—Na glanced shakily—"in her and tried to trap me. He wanted to steal my body. The woman, that poor woman, she's alive, but she's dead. He killed her." Tears fell onto Na's lap.

"And then?" Dr. Elmir pressed.

Na wiped her eyes. "Krasue kept coming after me, no matter where I was. I had to stop them both. So I tied them together. In the other world. Spiritually."

Taryn's face expressed pure bewilderment. Dr. Elmir patted her back. "Thank you, Taryn, for all of your help. I couldn't have found Rojana without you. Or you, Doug."

Doug lifted himself off the floor. "Na, I . . ." He reconsidered his phrasing and wiped his brow. "Yeah. Sure. This guy should have treated his employees better if he wanted to hide his secret, off-limits lab." Doug jingled a crowded keyring. "Especially from someone who knows most everyone in town." His demeanor changed back as he asked, "Um, Na? That was you, in the woman, then?"

"Yes."

"You looked a little like it. Krasue. Not like you," he stuttered. "Less, I don't know, healthy? Living?" Words poured out. "You were black and dead and I thought he'd killed you and we were hours too late. That I'd never get to hold you."

Na, spent and incapable of running to him, stayed silent on the bed and outstretched her arms. Doug walked to her and they embraced. *I missed you too.*

"Remember, we don't see everything here. This is the real world, right?" Dr. Elmir clarified. "That's just how it is. We can't really see what things look like until we're there ourselves. Na is fine, one hundred percent normal, right?"

Na smiled weakly in appreciation, uncertain whether Dr. Elmir believed what he said or if he was just being supportive. Maybe, by now, he'd reached the same conclusion as Saul, that she wasn't Rojana by birth. *I'll never know for sure, will I?*

A familiar jolt ran through Na's arm as a distant voice reverberated in Na's head: *Cotèl.* The Toulouse ghost took advantage of the relative peacefulness and shimmered into the room. Largely obscured by a bright ceiling light, just its faint outline was visible as it descended onto Taryn.

"No!" Na shouted. Doug and Dr. Elmir reflexively hopped backward.

It ignored Na and enveloped Taryn, crushing her onto the ground. Now a puppet master, it commanded her to grasp the scalpel and insulted them through her quaking lips: "Pecador! Pecador!"

Dr. Elmir latched on to Taryn to extricate her, momentarily stunning the specter. The Toulouse ghost fought back. It swung widely, slicing Dr. Elmir across his chest. Blood seeped through his split clothing.

Doug avoided the blade by tumbling sideways onto the wall and catching himself.

Na rose to meet the Toulouse attacker. Partially separating again by choice, she greeted the ghost on its own terms.

It hesitated. Its hollowed sockets eyed her carefully.

That's right. I'm like you. Better. Stronger. Na proclaimed her intention. *You*—she raised one hand toward it—*are next.* With the other hand, she aimed a finger at the wriggling Saul. *I'll make you like him.*

It did not reply. Na worried she had not projected her thoughts loudly or clearly enough to be heard. Instead, it froze. Then it responded by releasing Taryn. Before dissipating, it hissed once more, *Pecador. Cotèl.*

Once again, Na rejoined the living world. She put her arm around Taryn and helped her to her feet. Taryn gasped a few times and caught her breath. "I'm alright," Taryn said.

"My friends," Doug suggested, concerned about Dr. Elmir's wound, "the assistants. Take him to the assistants. They'll find nurses. They're not all bad. They're not part of this."

"Right." Taryn gave a thumbs-up. She put Dr. Elmir's arm over her back and, along with Doug, carried Dr. Elmir out of the room.

Whole, tired, and changed, Na sullenly shuffled behind them.

She did not spare an ounce of pity for Saul, who continued writhing, confined inside a self-contained prison.

EPILOGUE

ON THEIR PARTING, Dr. Elmir was not ready to leave Milton. He winked at Taryn and shook hands with Chief Rawls, saying, "Criminal investigations are out of my depth, and you've got a stack of cases to sort. I'll get out of your hair, at least for today. But I'm here if you need me for anything, and I'll return soon."

Later, during the first leg of their drive home, Na nagged him about not hugging Taryn. His excuse was the tender cut stitched closed across his chest.

Doug had not come to see them off, and Na did not blame him. Of course, he could have neglected Stuffs for just another couple of hours if he had wanted to, but both he and Na had a lot to unpack from the previous days. Dr. Elmir noted his absence and mentioned to Na that he planned to encourage Doug to attend their university.

That night, they stayed at the same halfway motel as they had before, on their way to Milton. Doug sent her a message: "Busy here but will text you later, k?"

Swiftly, Na replied, "Np. I'm here, only for you."

In the car for the second leg of their trip home, Dr. Elmir was less upbeat. "This is my fault, Na. I didn't imagine the possibility that you'd be put in danger like that. Or that my work could be abused in such a way. I'm thinking of changing my current academic focus, away from spiritual mechanics to an area less exploitable, like foreknowledge. That's an ability we saw no evidence of in Milton, right? And the university will provide you with counseling, as much as you need for as long as you need. Doug too. There's no shame in seeing a therapist, no matter what the issue is. I'm having nightmares of my own, and I witnessed less than half of what you did."

Lying on her back in her bedroom weeks later, her right arm heavily scarred but functionally recuperated, Na sketched, circled, and scribbled over courses she might want to take next quarter. *What now?* The registration deadline was nearing, and like it or not, she had reached the point in her education when she needed to decide what, or who, to become. *Scratch that. I know who I am. That bastard lied. Forget what he said.* What's more, it was impossible to keep her family safe from the threats she'd met; their menace was eternal. No degree kept demons at bay. *Never mind. I'll wait for Doug to get his schedule, take a course with him. Freshmen get priority registration. I'll talk to him tonight.* She grinned.

Na tossed the notepad onto her bed. *I can't delay choosing a major much longer, though. Maybe I'll know what to pick in an hour.* She sprang up from bed and yelled, "Mom, what are you cooking?"

THE END

Milton Keynes UK
Ingram Content Group UK Ltd.
UKHW011301210923
429112UK00001B/101

9 798888 240816